CW00597100

FEATHER & CLAW

MARTA PALAZZESI

FEATHER & CLAW

Illustrated by **Ambra Garlaschelli**
Translated by **Denise Muir**

First published in Great Britain in 2024 by
PICCADILLY PRESS
4th Floor, Victoria House, Bloomsbury Square, London WC1B 4DA
Owned by Bonnier Books, Sveavägen 56, Stockholm, Sweden
bonnierbooks.co.uk/Piccadilly Press

First published in Italian by Mondadori Libri S.p.A.

This book has been translated thanks to a translation grant awarded by the
Italian Ministry of Foreign Affairs and International Cooperation.
Questo libro è stato tradotto grazie a un contributo alla traduzione assegnato
dal Ministero degli Affari Esteri e della Cooperazione Internazionale
italiano.

A CIP catalogue record for this book is available from the British Library.

ISBN: 978-1-8007-8922-7
Also available as an ebook and in audio

1

Printed and bound in Great Britain by Clays Ltd, Elcograf S.p.A.

Piccadilly Press is an imprint of Bonnier Books UK
bonnierbooks.co.uk

PROLOGUE
Valencia, 1904

CHAPTER 1
Valencia, 1914

Amparo came hopping out of her bedroom, trying to tie the laces on her boots. The rush to move forward while jumping from one foot to another nearly sent her crashing to the ground, but she avoided it at the last minute by grabbing on to the shelf above the fireplace. She managed to right herself with one hand and without knocking over the row of tiny wooden animals she had painstakingly carved with an artistry that had gained the admiration of the entire *barrio*.

'I see someone's in a rush to get out,' commented her grandfather Mariano, who was sitting at the table, halfway through his daily ritual of filling his pipe and preparing to light it. A few strands of tobacco fell to the floor, landing on the fine layer of sawdust scattered across the bright pink and green tiles.

With her boots sorted, the young girl ran to the hook by the door and grabbed her green cape.

'I'll be back in an hour,' she announced and threw the cape around her shoulders.

Mariano agreed with a puff of his pipe. Two fine tendrils of smoke curled out of his nostrils, dancing in the warm air of the room.

'No going into the streets of El Cabanyal after dark though.'

'I know.'

'I know you know.' The man smiled. 'It's just that sometimes we forget what we know.'

Amparo bid her grandfather farewell and stepped out into the street. She wouldn't dare venture as far as the harbour in the dark, not even to see the fair that had recently come to town with its dozens of attractions, all carefully crafted to lure the public into their clutches then return them to the world with heads full of wonder and pockets full of air.

Don Sebastià, the old man who lived across the street from Amparo and her grandfather, was sitting on a chair outside his front door in the company of his giant black dog. Despite its fierce appearance, Tiano had the sweetest nature and would never dream of harming a soul – a fact Don Sebastià kept to himself and a few of his closest friends.

'Good evening, Don Sebastià,' Amparo said.

'Good evening, little Amparo,' replied the man, who was only a few years younger than Amparo's grandfather and had lived alone for as long as she had known him.

Tiano got up from his master's feet to greet the young girl, who gave him a friendly ruffle and rub of the ears. The dog barked, causing a couple of passing pedlars to jump in fright and hurry on past.

Don Sebastià sneered. 'That'll teach them to come hawking their wares here.'

Amparo gave the dog one last rub and planted a kiss on its silky snout. 'See you later, lovely. Bye, Don Sebastià.'

'Goodbye, dear.'

A few doors down from her neighbour, the girl came across the local beggar, currently fast asleep, who was always in that same spot. She scooted past and hurried on down the alleyway. The solid, square bell tower of San Bartolomeo came into view at the end, and she could just about make out a group of drunk men huddled at its feet. Amparo was making her way past them when the caretaker of the building opposite, one of the many that had polished wooden gates and wrought-iron balconies, emerged shaking a broom in his hand.

'Get out of here! Be off with you, beggars!' he ordered.

Amparo hurried on, hoping to escape the impending brawl. Leaving the bell tower behind, she came to the junction with the bright and lively street, Calle Caballeros. Music and laughter, not to mention a myriad of tempting smells, burst forth from its taverns. Forcing down the hunger pangs, she kept walking, reflecting on what she'd seen earlier that day when she'd flown over the fair. A lot of the attractions had been closed, although not the Hall of Mirrors or the Haunted House. She'd perched nearby, studying the expressions on the fairgoers' faces as they had emerged from these places: a mix of fear, fun and disappointment, perhaps from having spent so much money and having had such high hopes for something so ephemeral.

As she came to the end of Calle Caballeros, the cathedral came into view. The square in front of it was crowded with people who had come to admire the wooden figures of Mary and baby Jesus. In a few days' time, these would be covered with flowers as Valencia's city-wide festival – Las Fallas – got into full swing. Amparo adored this celebration, not just for the firework displays and the array of lights and tapestry of colourful bunting and murals decorating the streets. She especially liked the colossal wooden sculptures that would pop up all over the city to then be ritually set on fire on the night of March 19th. Only the winning sculptures would be saved. This year, their local *phalera* committee had asked her grandfather to be part of the Barrio del Carmen preparations and Amparo hoped with all her heart that they would win one of the prizes.

'Well, look who it is.'

'Look how lily white she is.'

'What do you expect, spends all her time cooped up at home, she does. We're not worthy of her company any more. Stuck-up little madam.'

Despite all the noise and revelry around her, Amparo could still make out the voices of Emilia, Renata and Mirela. They were behind her; all she had to do was turn around and she could confront them. She chose not to. After all, she would've thought the same if she were in their shoes. If one of her friends had stopped answering the door, she would have called her a stuck-up madam too. Maybe worse.

The story Mariano had put around was that his granddaughter had developed a strange allergy to the sun. While it may have been believed by most adults who had too much respect for her grandfather and his work to question him, the young weren't so easily fooled.

Amparo pushed her shoulders back, held her head high, picked up her pace and left her old friends behind. She went past a group of tourists speaking a language she didn't understand then swerved a cluster of stalls.

'Hey, pretty girl, let me read your future!' a fortune teller called from a nearby stall draped in dark purple velvet.

Amparo shook her head. The woman seemed keen on offering her services anyway. She shuffled the cards between long fingers with red-painted nails and pulled out three cards, which she kept hidden.

'Ah,' she mumbled, raising her eyebrows. 'Interesting.'

In spite of herself, Amparo slowed down. Eyes twinkling shrewdly, the fortune teller hinted at another revelation.

'A secret. A return. A vendetta,' she declared. 'Wouldn't you like to know more?'

With a shrug of the shoulders and a fleeting smile, Amparo went on her way. She'd grown up among the cacophony of voices ringing through the Barrio del Carmen: the calls of street traders peddling *horchata*, the babble of conversations between women travelling home from market, the shrill cries of children, the hushed whispering of nuns, the honeyed tones of street hustlers, the velvety-soft voices of fortune tellers and crystal-ball gazers, telling mostly the same things, hinting at distant loves, dark enemies and indecipherable mysteries.

Yet, as she walked away with her back straight and her head held high, merging with the crowds in the square, she felt a tingle run down her spine. Like a prickle, it was as if the invisible hand of fate were trying to tell her that, perhaps, the fortune teller's words might have held some truth.

CHAPTER 2

The sunset caught her unawares.

By the time she felt the customary tingling in her wings, it was too late. She tried to fly away, to seek cover, but the light, feathered body of the falcon was about to give way to the heavier, less mobile body of a human.

Amparo floundered, gasping for air, reached out to grab the fabric of the tent as she began slipping down the slope, her previous sharp, hooked claws replaced with short, smooth nails. Useless.

She tumbled head over heels to the ground.

'Aargh!' she cried, dazed, confused . . . and angry. How could she have been so reckless? Transforming outside the safety of her home, where anyone could have seen her.

The reason was obvious though: never in her life had she met someone like him.

The world might think it had just witnessed the most amazing sleight of hand, or even that the boy had literally vanished under a trapdoor or behind a mirror, but she knew the truth: the boy and the panther were one and the same. Just like her and the falcon.

Don't think about that now, she said to herself, scrambling to her feet. *You need to find clothes first and get out of here.*

So far, she hadn't had much luck, but good fortune hadn't abandoned her completely. When she'd fallen, she'd tumbled into the narrow gap between two tents, the Magic Lair on one side – from which much shouting and rowdy applause were emanating – and a smaller, quieter tent on the other.

It would be good if it was empty.

She felt her way along the tent wall, seeking a gap or a way in, but the fabric seemed to be held tautly to the ground by a series of enormous wooden pegs. Just when it seemed she'd be stuck there for the night, Amparo spotted one peg slightly higher in the ground than the others. Hopeful, she grabbed the top of it and started to pull, ignoring the splinters that jagged her hands.

The peg eventually gave way and, with a sigh of relief, Amparo snuck into the dark, quiet tent.

A store, she realised. *There have to be some clothes in here. Or a blanket at least.*

She couldn't see anything that might be suitable, partly because it was too dark to see properly and partly because it was such a mess. There were stage backdrops piled precariously on top of one another, wagon wheels with flaking paint, stuffed birds in cages, which sent shivers down her spine, papier-mâché dolls and puppets with broken arms; the silent victims of the antics of some capricious child. Stacks of crates and boxes rose from the ground like wobbly sugar spires.

Amparo moved silently through the dust-filled battle-field, trying not to bump into anything. A few minutes later, she came across a rack of clothes peeping out from behind a mirror-clad cart. She darted round it, averting her eyes from her reflection, and began sifting through the clothes, looking for something that might fit. They were all men's stage costumes – long, brocade cloaks, thick, multicoloured jackets, wide, tasselled breeches: nothing for a girl of her slim build. It was then that she spotted a black and white striped fabric. She pulled at it and found herself holding a pair of skinny trousers with gold buttons.

They must've been for a child, she thought to herself as she pulled them on. They reached no further than halfway down her calves, but she was hardly going to meet the crowds in Plaza de la Reina. She just needed to cover up, in whatever way she could. She rummaged a little more, hunting for a blouse or a shirt she could wear, but the only thing of any use was a long black gilet with ornamental frogging on the front. She pulled it on then tied a red scarf she'd also found around her waist.

She looked ridiculous, but at least she was clothed.

Gingerly, she made her way back out, pushing the tent flap aside, and found herself in the midst of a stream of people, swarming along the main avenue of the fairground. She heaved a sigh of relief: no one would notice her in this big a crowd. At worst, they'd think she was an acrobat.

Emerging from her hiding place, she set off along the avenue, zigzagging this way and that around well-dressed couples with children in tow (albeit under the ever watchful eye of obligatory nannies) or more modest folks dawdling along with their heads bent back as they gazed, transfixed, at the myriad lights and spectacles around them. Swarms of noisy children darted here and there; pickpockets – who Amparo had learned to recognise at an early age – loitered in the long shadows between attractions, lying in wait for their next victim.

She went under the large illuminated archway and entered El Cabanyal, hurrying, head down, anxious to get home. A horse-drawn omnibus clanked past her and she wondered if they'd let her on, despite not having the money for a ticket. She got her answer a mere second later when a barefoot and filthy young boy was kicked off the moving bus by an irate conductor.

The boy tumbled to the ground but bounced back up quickly, shaking a fist at the man while hurling a barrage of insults. The attack ended with a rude gesture that Amparo couldn't help herself but comment on.

'What's it to you?' the boy shouted back. 'Look at you, did you just escape from the convent school for the poor?' He was as thin as a rake with dark bushy eyebrows and a mop of tangled hair. He looked like one of the emaciated cats that lurked around the Barrio del Carmen, thin but as tough as old boots and clearly afraid of nothing.

For a second, Amparo envied him.

Evidently unaware of Amparo's silent admiration, the boy aimed a loud raspberry at her, then followed it up with an insult as vulgar as the rude gesture he'd made earlier. Then he disappeared as quick as a whip into the alleyways of El Cabanyal.

Amparo didn't move, still reeling from the encounter, until a burst of shouting behind her broke her reverie. Focused again, she hurried on.

Outside the many inns along the way, groups of drunk men roared boorishly while wily hustlers tried to trick them in the game of three cards. Amparo went past a hastily erected stall where a man was moving walnut shells around in front of bleary-eyed spectators.

The long avenue came to an end in a large square, illuminated by a solitary flickering street light in the centre. Three boys loitered below it. Amparo stopped short, sensing danger. Too late. The boys were nudging each other, having already noticed her. They were bigger and much heftier than Amparo. Running away wasn't an option, they'd only set upon her like prey. So she squared her shoulders and kept going, planning to cross the square.

The boys sniggered as she went past.

'Would you look at this freak here,' the beefiest boy of the group commented.

'That a boy or a girl?' asked one of the others.

She ignored them, feeling even more at risk now they were behind her.

'Hey, you! Stop right there!' they yelled.

Amparo kept walking, but the blow struck her between the shoulder blades. She stifled a scream as the bottle thrown at her shattered into pieces on the ground, cutting her feet.

She whirled around, furious, saw the three of them striding towards her, sneering.

'This is our turf,' the heavyset boy declared. 'You need to pay a toll.'

'Empty your pockets,' the second boy ordered. 'Or we'll do it for you.'

'I don't have any money,' Amparo replied. 'And even if I did, I certainly wouldn't give it to you lot.'

The three boys burst out laughing.

'Ooh, bit of a sharp tongue we have here,' the biggest boy said, clearly the leader of the group. A knife appeared from the sleeve of his grimy shirt. 'Come over here and I'll cut it off for you. Ow!' The boy suddenly collapsed to his knees, groaning in pain, while from behind him the thin, insult-hurling boy who'd been thrown off the bus earlier popped out.

'Scum,' the big boy cursed. 'Wait till I get my hands on you . . .'

But the new arrival didn't waste any time in delivering another blow to the boy on the ground and when the other two attempted to stop him, he kicked one of them hard on the shins and sunk his teeth into the hand of the third one.

'Aaargh!' the latter wailed, trying to shake the young boy off.

The little biter wouldn't let go, not until the boy began to beg.

'Stop. Stop, please. You'll have it off if you don't stop!'

The young boy spat out the hand of his victim. 'You need to wash more often, Gonzalo. You taste like dead fish.' Then he spun his stick in the air above his head. 'Now beat it! Unless you want to lose your fingers!'

The three boys retreated.

'You're dead, Pepe,' the biggest one threatened.

Pepe spat at him. 'You're no more than a diseased dog, Cayetano. Three of you, picking on a girl! Go on, get lost!'

Unbelievably, they ran away.

'Spineless cowards,' Pepe spluttered, shaking his head. 'Disgusting, filthy cowards . . .'

Amparo cleared her throat and her unlikely saviour turned to her. 'What are you still doing here? Are you waiting for them to come back? What's your problem, hanging around here alone at this time of night, you're not very bright, are you?'

Amparo bristled at the insult, but she had to accept he wasn't wrong.

'Pepe, is that your name?'

'You're quick, eh?' He laughed. 'Yes, my name's Pepe. And you are?'

'Amparo.'

'Hmm,' he muttered, looking her up and down. 'You're the girl from before. You work at the fair?'

'No. I came to see the shows and stayed a bit too late.'

Pepe scratched his shin with one of his bare feet and through his tattered clothes, Amparo glimpsed the skinny, almost emaciated body, skin brown from both the sun and dirt.

'Yes, I've never seen you around here before,' he remarked. 'Anyway, don't listen to that idiot Cayetano, this isn't his turf, it's mine: I'm the king of El Cabanyal.'

'Seriously?' Amparo couldn't help asking, sceptical.

'Of course,' Pepe responded in all seriousness. 'My family run a very famous *tienda*, I'll have you know. They sell all sorts of delicious things, people come from all over the city. If you ever feel like a proper *jamón*, just pay us a visit. Oh, but be careful if it's my brother Enrique behind the counter. The minute he sees someone like you, he'll kick you out without as much as a second word. Papa, on the other hand, is much kinder to orphans.'

'How do you do know . . .' Amparo began.

'Well, it's obvious, isn't it?' Pepe interrupted. 'You're

dressed like that and you're wandering around El Cabanyal alone after dark. You've obviously got no one waiting for you at home.'

'I do so,' Amparo replied. 'My grandad.'

'What about your parents?'

'Both dead,' Amparo confessed.

Pepe smiled. 'See? I was right. You *are* an orphan.'

She scowled. 'That's not very kind.'

With a shrug the boy replied, 'It's the world that's unkind, not me. So it's just you and your grandfather at home?'

Amparo nodded.

'That must be really boring. There are nine of us in my house: my dad, my seven brothers: Enrique, Bartomeu, Nofrem, Geroni, Pere, Guillem, Alonso, then me. I'm the youngest but also the smartest.'

And the gobbiest, thought Amparo. 'What about your mum?' she asked.

'She died. Years ago. I don't remember her.'

Pepe pointed to his threadbare shirt with a smile, revealing a mouthful of inexplicably white teeth. 'This was Enrique's when he was my age. Which means it's . . .' he seemed to be racking his brain, totting up the numbers, 'it's from 1897. How about that? My shirt's from last century!'

He seemed to find this greatly amusing and started cackling. Amparo couldn't help but smile: Pepe looked like an underfed cat, but the noise he was making was more like a braying mule.

'Well,' Pepe resumed. 'I'll say goodbye now. I have a lot to do tonight.' He cast a doubtful eye over Amparo. 'Are you sure you'll make it home in one piece?'

Amparo nodded, more out of pride than conviction.

Pepe clicked his tongue to bid her farewell then strode back into the dark shadows of El Cabanyal.

CHAPTER 3

When Amparo got home, she found Mariano waiting for her in the candlelit kitchen, a serious look on his face and a pipe in his mouth. She closed the door quietly behind her and looked straight at him in silence.

'I will not scold you nor will you be punished,' he began. 'I think you know yourself how dangerous what you have just done is.'

Amparo nodded. She felt terrible, ashamed – even more so because of her grandfather's quiet, calm voice. The old man was right of course.

'I want to know more about my parents,' she exclaimed. 'You always refuse to talk about them but I *need* to know.'

Mariano remained impassive, showing no sign of responding to his granddaughter's request. 'I have told you everything there is to know, Amparo. They died when you were very young, at . . .'

'At sea,' Amparo snapped. 'Yes, you said, but is that really true? Did they really drown?'

Looking worried, Mariano asked, 'Where do all these doubts come from?' He dipped his pipe towards the young girl's clothing. 'Does it have something to do with your night-time trip to the fair?'

Amparo shrugged. 'No, it's just you never talk about them.'

'I don't speak about them because there's not much to say.'

Amparo went to open her mouth to complain, but Mariano continued decisively, 'Except that they loved you a lot.'

Amparo decided to let it go, realising her grandfather wouldn't say any more. She wasn't ready to share what she'd seen yet, even less so discuss all the confusing images – of fire and smoke – that her encounter with the panther-boy had reawakened in her mind.

Everyone has secrets, she realised. *I should know that more than most*, she thought to herself.

The girl nodded. 'Yes, I understand.' She walked over to the stairs. 'Goodnight, grandfather.'

'Goodnight.'

Amparo felt her grandfather's gaze shadow her upstairs. She dared not breathe as she climbed the steps, scared he'd forbid her from going out after sunset or want to know more about why she'd been so late. Mariano did neither of these things though, so when Amparo was finally alone in her room, she heaved a long sigh of relief.

She lay down on the bed and closed her eyes. She wasn't sure what it was that bothered her more: discovering someone else like her or the fact that the unexpected encounter had reawakened memories she didn't know she had.

'Fire and smoke . . .'

She was sure she'd never been in a fire. At least not since she'd been living with her grandfather, a carpenter who feared fire more than anything else.

So where could those mixed-up images have come from? From when she was tiny and still living with her parents?

How could they be connected to the boy who she was sure she'd never met before?

Amparo knew there was only one way to find out: she had to speak to him.

But even if the boy were only half as suspicious of strangers as she was, and half as protective of his secret, that wasn't going to be easy.

Mariano pushed open Amparo's half-open bedroom door, stepping cautiously into her room.

'I'm off to Donna Consuelo's tavern for dinner. Do you want to join me?'

Amparo was sitting at her desk. She shook her head. 'I ate earlier.'

'Are you sure?'

The girl looked up from the paper, lips curving into a smile. In the flickering light of the oil lamp, the old man's face looked tired and ridged with deep furrows. Amparo couldn't help but feel guilty for the worry she'd caused him the night before.

Another reason not to tell him anything.

'Yes, I'm sure,' she replied resolutely.

His lips pressed into a thin line behind the grey beard, squashing any doubts with a puff on his pipe, Mariano said, 'All right. See you later.'

Once her grandfather had gone, Amparo looked back at the letter. She knew exactly what she wanted to say but not quite how to say it. The last thing she wanted was to frighten the panther-boy – Tomás he was called – or for him to feel threatened by her. But she had to give him a reason to come out into the open and meet her.

Eventually, she decided to simply suggest a meeting time and place. Gazing at the ink as it dried, she added one final thing:

I am Feather.

She slipped the sheet of paper into an envelope, opened the small door on the lamp and held a block of wax over the flame. When it had softened, she closed the envelope, but before sealing it she picked up the white feather lying beside the inkwell – it had fallen out earlier – and popped it inside the envelope before finally pressing down on the wax to seal it. She blew on it to dry the wax quicker, flipped the envelope over and wrote *For Claw* in one corner.

He'll understand, she said to herself as she stood up.

The letter tucked into her dress pocket, she went downstairs and pulled on the cape she'd left on the chair beside the fire. She checked all the windows were shut – there'd been quite a few break-ins recently in the *barrio* – then left the house, pulling the heavy wooden door shut behind her. She lingered briefly on the doorstep, thinking. She had to go back to El Cabanyal to leave the note for Tomás, no doubt about that, but it also put her at risk of being attacked by Cayetano and his henchmen, or some other miscreant out on the streets at night.

'Woof!'

Jumping up from where he'd been lying at his master's feet, Tiano bounded over to Amparo and nuzzled his head against her legs. She ruffled his ears and received a series of contented whimpers back. An idea occurred to her.

'Don Sebastià, would you mind if I take Tiano for a walk?'

Sitting on his usual straw-seated wooden chair, the man waved a hand good-naturedly. 'Of course, off you go. Poor creature, I'm too old now for the long walks along the beach I used to take him on.'

'Here, lovely,' Amparo said as the dog fell in by her side, wagging its tail happily.

With Tiano as bodyguard, no one would dare approach her, even less so bother her. The massive hulk of a canine, with his black coat and large orange eyes, looked more like a beast risen from hell come to wreak terror on Las Fallas than a simple pet.

The pair made their way across the city, passing through the centre and its many iconic squares and streets – the elegant Plaza de la Reina, the vibrant Plaza del Ayuntamiento, and the wide, tree-lined Via del Marqués del Turia – until they finally crossed the river and its dark water.

'Keep going, Tiano,' Amparo urged. 'Not far now.'

The dog didn't seem at all bothered by the length of the journey. Quite the opposite. He trotted along merrily beside his temporary master, stopping every now and then to sniff a lamppost and, where necessary, leave evidence of his passage.

Amparo and Tiano followed the river upstream a few hundred metres, as far as the imposing Puente del Mar, which was crowded with a constant stream of night-time trams, carriages and festivalgoers.

'Stay close, Tiano,' Amparo said, resting a hand on the dog's back. They stayed as close as they could to the low stone balustrade to avoid being run over by the moving vehicles.

When they finally reached El Cabanyal, the night sky unfurled above them like a stretch of black velvet, its inky depths occasionally pierced by bursts of light from the fair. They turned down the avenue that led to the attractions, passing under the arches of lights that towered above them.

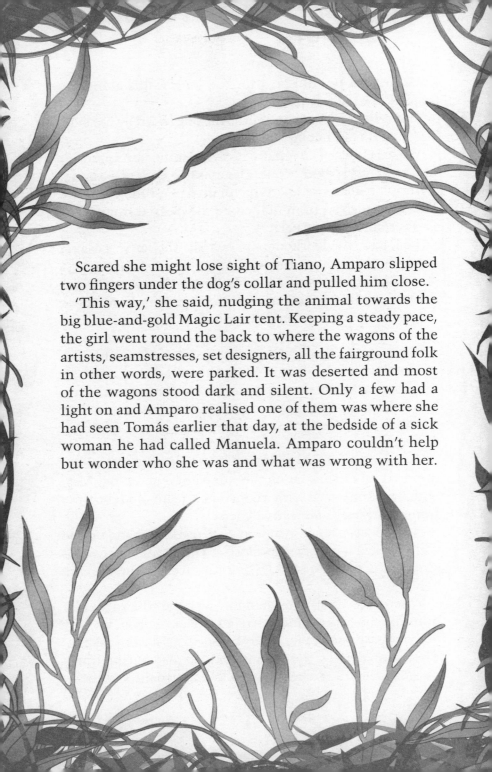

Scared she might lose sight of Tiano, Amparo slipped two fingers under the dog's collar and pulled him close.

'This way,' she said, nudging the animal towards the big blue-and-gold Magic Lair tent. Keeping a steady pace, the girl went round the back to where the wagons of the artists, seamstresses, set designers, all the fairground folk in other words, were parked. It was deserted and most of the wagons stood dark and silent. Only a few had a light on and Amparo realised one of them was where she had seen Tomás earlier that day, at the bedside of a sick woman he had called Manuela. Amparo couldn't help but wonder who she was and what was wrong with her.

Beside the woman's wagon was the one Tomás used, a little smaller than the rest, but unlike the others, adorned with an impressive mural of a sleek black panther with piercing green eyes.

Tiano followed Amparo meekly over to the painted wagon although she sensed tension in the dog. It seemed to be on high alert, tail straight up, ears pricked and head bobbing nervously this way and that.

'Don't worry, Tiano, everything's fine.'

Amparo climbed the wooden steps up to the wagon's door and nudged it slowly open. The hinges creaked. She hurried inside, quickly located Tomás's bed, crept over and slipped the envelope under his pillow. Aware she could be caught any minute, she couldn't help but stop to admire all the pictures pinned on the walls of the wagon.

He's quite an artist, this guy, she thought to herself, in awe of the meticulously crafted portraits before her, so richly detailed that she wouldn't have been surprised if the subjects had actually spoken to her. She could see in these drawings the same care she put into the sketches she herself made before carving a piece of wood.

A noise outside snapped her attention back from the paintings. Quick as lightning, she went outside, shut the door and tiptoed down the steps.

You made it, she congratulated herself. *Here's hoping Tomás agrees to meet you.*

'Let's go, Tiano.'

Amparo walked away, but after a few steps, she realised the big black dog seemed to have no intention of moving.

'Grrr.'

'Come here, Tiano!' she hissed nervously. 'There's no one there!'

She was under no illusion though. If an animal senses danger, it's very rarely wrong.

A shadow flitted between the two wagons.

'I was told you were wandering around with the devil's very own mastiff in tow, and blow me down if it isn't true!'

A grinning Pepe emerged from the shadows.

'You were told?' Amaro queried.

'I'm the king of El Cabanyal,' the boy replied. 'Nothing gets past me. Does that thing bite?'

Amparo looked at Tiano. The dog, deeming Pepe to be harmless, had switched off his alert mode and was now merrily wagging its tail.

'No.'

'Thank goodness for that,' Pepe remarked, stepping closer to the dog. 'Just as well, he wouldn't find much to sink his teeth into. Come over here, handsome, give us a cuddle.'

Pepe gave the dog a vigorous rub and the dog responded so enthusiastically he sent the poor boy flying.

'You really are a devil, aren't you?' Pepe said, picking himself back up with a smile on his face. He seemed used to falling down. 'So what are you doing round these parts again?' he asked Amparo.

The girl shrugged. 'Nothing.'

'You didn't walk halfway across the city, in the dark, with this big beast in tow for "nothing",' Pepe retorted. He clocked Tomás's wagon. 'Might it have something to do with that?'

'No,' Amparo flatly denied the suggestion and turned to walk away with Tiano.

'I'll find out, you know,' said Pepe, falling in behind her. 'You might as well just tell me now.'

Amparo ignored him and walked out on to the main avenue through the fair, hoping Pepe would give up as they headed into the crowds.

The boy stuck to his guns and the next thing Amparo

knew, Pepe had fallen into step with her and was now by her side.

'You were holding something when you went inside that wagon,' he commented. 'What was it?'

'Nothing,' she repeated, obstinate. 'Tiano, come closer.'

The dog nuzzled her side and Amparo put an arm around his neck to pull him even closer.

'Come on, don't make me beg. You're not very . . .' But before he could finish, Pepe was cut short when Amparo, in a fit of anger, gave him an almighty shove.

'Leave me alone!'

'Ouch!' Pepe exclaimed, taken by surprise. He rubbed his arm and looked menacingly at Amparo. Tiano, despite the cuddles he had accepted earlier, rushed to the girl's defence, snarling at the king of El Cabanyal.

'You haven't heard the last of this,' Pepe grumbled angrily before disappearing into the crowds.

Amparo stood rooted to the spot for a few seconds, feeling a little guilty but also a little relieved. There was a reason she'd cut off all ties with her old friends since she'd discovered what she was. She'd rather shut down contact with people from the get-go, certain that as soon as they learned her secret, they wouldn't want to be anywhere near someone like her.

And I definitely wasn't making an exception for that Pepe, she told herself.

Resolute, she grabbed Tiano's collar and set off towards home, leaving the fair behind her.

CHAPTER 4

One full day had gone past since Amparo had left the note for Tomás. A day that had been full of doubts and torment. Nevertheless, the much hoped-for moment eventually arrived: she would soon find out if the boy had decided to meet her.

The meeting place was not too far from the fairground, in a no man's land of sorts, neither beach nor field, a barren stretch of ground inhabited only by stray dogs and passing seagulls.

Amparo was so nervous she barely slept and ended up getting up much earlier than planned. She dressed silently in the dark, ears pricked for any noise. The only one she heard though was the deep, rhythmic snoring of her grandfather, which rumbled around the house like the great, gusty bellows of a sleeping giant.

Amparo padded softly down the stairs, pulled on her cape and checked her pockets to make sure she had everything she needed. She left a note for her grandfather on the kitchen table, telling him she'd be back after breakfast. Then she left.

The windows in Don Sebastià's house were all dark, Amparo pictured the old man fast asleep in his bed, the faithful Tiano watching over him. She strode down the alley at a brisk pace, walking past the same corpulent beggar who muttered something before drifting off back to sleep under his frayed and tattered cloak.

It wasn't yet dawn but the *barrio* was already buzzing with activity: boys on bikes delivering bread, maids carrying baskets filled with bottles of fresh milk, craftsmen hurrying to their workshops, festivalgoers on their way home after a night of revelry.

It took Amparo only a few minutes to reach Plaza de la Reina, which was still slumbering in the shadow of the cathedral. She headed straight for a row of carriages for hire.

'Sir, can you take me to El Cabanyal, please?'

Up in the box, the driver, a lanky man wrapped in a heavy cloth coat was busy tucking into his breakfast. Rolling his eyes, he looked down at Amparo.

'Why on earth would a girl like you be wanting to go to El Cabanyal? Go back to bed and let me finish my food in peace.'

'But . . .'

'I'll take you to El Cabanyal,' piped up the driver of the next carriage, a youngish-looking man with a tired but kind face. 'I've finished for tonight and am heading home to my wife and son. I can take you to the start of Playa de la Malvarrosa, will that do?'

'Amazing,' Amparo replied, heaving a sigh of relief. 'That's exactly where I'm going.'

'I can't imagine why,' muttered the first coachman, shrugging his shoulders. 'You should be home in bed, if you ask me.'

Ignoring him, Amparo climbed into the carriage of the younger man, who cracked his whip and set the wheels in motion. This trip was going to cost Amparo her entire savings but to go back into El Cabanyal on foot without Tiano was just too dangerous. What's more, she couldn't risk getting to the appointment after dawn. That was out of the question.

The carriage left the narrow city streets, crossed the river and turned on to the Paseo al Mar, a long, tree-lined road connecting the city to the harbour and the beach. In the distance, Amparo could make out the dark outline of the fair; further still, the glimmering lights of the port, seemingly swaying in time to the oscillating masts of the ships in harbour.

'We're here.'

The coachman's muffled voice broke through the silence from outside. The horses had come to a stop by the sand so Amparo opened the door of the carriage and jumped out, sending a cloud of dust swirling up from the ground.

She slipped a hand into her pocket. 'Your money, sir.'

The man shook his head. 'Keep it for the return trip. And be careful. Promise?'

She nodded. 'Thank you.'

The carriage pulled away, wobbling as it moved over the uneven ground, and made its way towards the port. Amparo gazed in the opposite direction, towards the fair, which was shrouded in dark and silence, and hesitated as she noticed the eerily dark strip behind it. A cold breeze with a stinging chill swept off the water, ruffling her hair. She felt a tingling run down her spine again, like fate warning her, trying desperately to divert her from her current course of action. Amparo ignored it and strode firmly forward towards her meeting.

The desolate expanse of land before her was deserted. In the centre stood an old votive shrine with a few seagulls perched on it. Amparo drew her cape tighter around her neck and focused her attention on the shrine, wondering if the panther had already arrived.

The gulls wouldn't be so quiet if he had.

She reached the shrine and looked around. A strip of orange coloured the horizon, signalling that dawn would arrive soon. Why hadn't Tomás come?

'Who is Claw?'

Amparo jumped as a thin figure approached.

'You again?!' she shrieked.

The king of El Cabanyal stopped in front of her, hands in his trouser pockets and an inquisitive look on his dusty face.

'You are Feather, that's obvious,' Pepe continued. 'What I don't get is who Claw is.'

'Well, the thing *I* don't get is what you, of all people, are doing *here*?' Amparo shouted. 'Would you just go away?!'

'Not a chance,' Pepe replied, not batting an eyelid. 'I want to know what you're up to on my patch.'

'You read . . .'

'. . . the note you left in that wagon. Yes, of course I did,' Pepe cut her off brusquely. 'And it doesn't matter if you don't tell me who Claw is, I'm going to find out soon anyway,' he stated calmly, leaning on the shrine, arms folded.

'Now you listen to me,' Amparo began, struggling to stifle her anger. She needed to think clearly: she'd have a chance to take Pepe to task for going through Tomás's wagon later; for now, she just needed to get rid of him. 'You can't be here with me. It's dangerous.'

'Dangerous?' laughed Pepe. 'What am I supposed to be afraid of? You?'

'Grrr.'

The panther took them by surprise from behind. At first, Amparo could only make out the glint of its green eyes, glowing in the first light of dawn. Then she saw the rest: the

powerful paws, the arched back, the gracefully curving tail.

Pepe let forth a strangled cry as he implored the mercy of the Almighty.

'I told you,' admonished Amparo with a note of satisfaction.

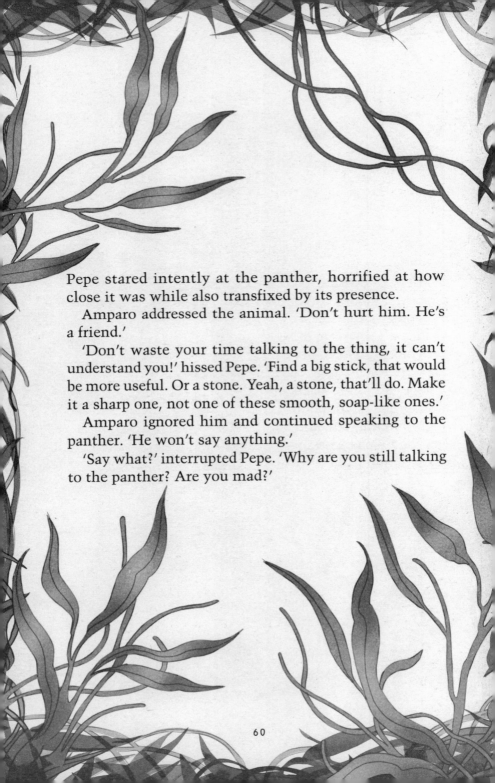

Pepe stared intently at the panther, horrified at how close it was while also transfixed by its presence.

Amparo addressed the animal. 'Don't hurt him. He's a friend.'

'Don't waste your time talking to the thing, it can't understand you!' hissed Pepe. 'Find a big stick, that would be more useful. Or a stone. Yeah, a stone, that'll do. Make it a sharp one, not one of these smooth, soap-like ones.'

Amparo ignored him and continued speaking to the panther. 'He won't say anything.'

'Say what?' interrupted Pepe. 'Why are you still talking to the panther? Are you mad?'

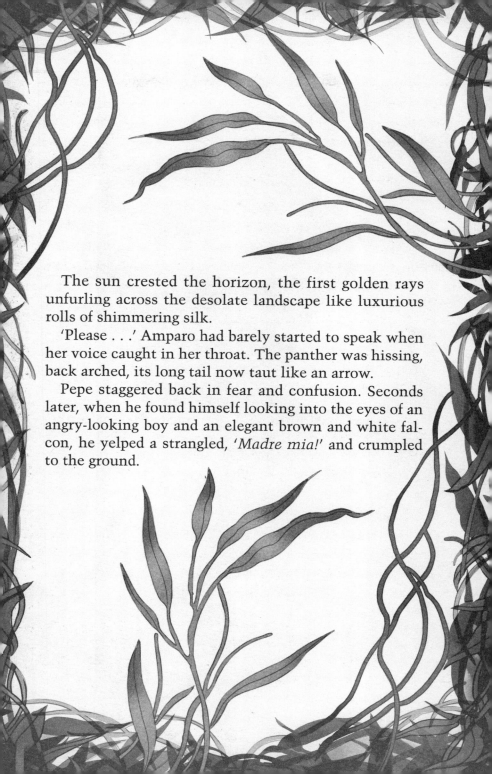

The sun crested the horizon, the first golden rays unfurling across the desolate landscape like luxurious rolls of shimmering silk.

'Please . . .' Amparo had barely started to speak when her voice caught in her throat. The panther was hissing, back arched, its long tail now taut like an arrow.

Pepe staggered back in fear and confusion. Seconds later, when he found himself looking into the eyes of an angry-looking boy and an elegant brown and white falcon, he yelped a strangled, '*Madre mia!*' and crumpled to the ground.

Tomás yanked Pepe by the shirt. 'Don't say a word or you're dead. Do you understand?'

'But you . . . But she . . .' Pepe stammered, still gasping for breath and eyes wide. 'But how . . . ?'

Tomás dragged Pepe to his feet, ripped his tattered shirt from him and used it to tie the urchin up. Pepe was so shocked he offered no resistance. Once immobilised, Tomás shoved him back to the ground.

It was only then that he glanced disapprovingly at the falcon, which was perched on the shrine having gotten rid of the seagulls. He showed no sign of surprise at the girl's transformation. If anything, the situation just looked like a major inconvenience to him, nothing else.

Tomás walked over to the shrine, reached behind the statue of the Virgin Mary and pulled out a ball of bundled-up clothes. He dressed quickly, switching his glare between the falcon and Pepe as he pulled on a shirt and trousers.

'I guess he wasn't part of the plan,' he grumbled, picking up Amparo's clothes and rummaging through the pockets of her sage-coloured cape.

'How very predictable, Feather,' he commented when he came across an envelope. He opened it and read the note inside. Then he looked up from the paper and gazed intently at the falcon. 'You're wrong.'

The raptor screeched. Pepe, curled up on the ground, pleaded for the compassion of any random saint that might be listening.

Tomás shook his head and the orange dawn light caught his dark hair, turning it into a shimmering cascade of copper gold.

'The woman who brought me up, Manuela, told me she found me when I was four years old. wandering on a beach in Barcelona. I have nothing to do with the fire you remember. Or with . . .' Tomás looked down at Amparo's letter, 'a burning tower.' In pronouncing these final words though, his voice faltered, as if struck by a sudden realisation.

The falcon twitched nervously and gave a second squawk. Tomás stood, immobile, for a long time, staring at Amparo's words as the sea breeze began to whip around them again. In the distance, dogs barked.

'P-p-pardon me,' Pepe broke in, 'but . . . this burning tower you both remember . . .'

Tomás shook his head firmly. 'I don't remember any burning tower.'

'Well, she does though,' Pepe fired back, his normal bravado slowly returning. 'And there was a tower here in Valencia, on the Trastamara estate . . .' he cleared his voice and sat down, 'which burned down about ten years ago.'

With a beat of its wings, the falcon flew off the roof of the shrine and swooped down on to Pepe's knees, which he had crossed in front of him. He gasped.

'Don't take my eyes out!'

Tomás laughed. 'You're a bit chicken to be the king of El Cabanyal!'

'Well, I'll have you know, I deal with thugs and thiefs, criminals and swindlers every day, just not . . .'

The look on Tomás's face hardened. 'Not what? Go on, say it. Tell us what we are.'

'I don't know what you are,' replied Pepe. 'I don't judge. So don't mock me for being afraid. For the love of God, you were a panther until just five minutes ago! And she . . . she was a girl and now she's a bird!'

'A falcon. She's a falcon,' Tomás corrected.

Pepe shook his head. 'All right, all right, a falcon,' he mumbled. 'How many more are there, like you, around?'

'I have no idea,' replied Tomás. 'Until I met her, I thought I was the only one.'

'You don't seem too happy to have found another,' Pepe remarked.

'Should I be?'

'Er, I don't know. I would've thought . . .'

'I wouldn't wish this life on anyone,' Tomás snapped. 'So no, I'm not happy.' He fell silent for a bit. 'Tell me about the Trastamara estate.'

'It burned down ten years ago.'

'You said that already. What else?'

'Right, let me see.' Pepe closed his eyes. 'It belonged to a very wealthy man, Don Ricardo Trastamara. He built palaces for rich folk like him, but he didn't treat his workers very well. Rumour has it they set fire to the estate.'

Tomás raised his eyebrows. Pepe hurried on.

'His wife was beautiful but also a bit incapaciferous . . .'

'Incapaciferous? Do you maybe mean incapacitated?'

Pepe shrugged. 'Yeah, whatever, she was always poorly. She wasn't from around here though. Don Trastamara supposedly brought her back from some cold country up north.'

Tomás's brow furrowed deeper. 'Keep going.'

Pepe was deep in concentration, as if trawling the depths of his memory for any local rumours and gossip that might have been stored there over the years.

'She couldn't have children, not to begin with anyway,' the king of El Cabanyal continued. 'Now don't ask me why, because what would I know about this sort of stuff? I'm hardly a wet nurse now, am I?'

'I can see that. Keep going,' Tomás prompted, growing impatient.

'Well, out of the blue, a child appeared. The gossip was that Don Trastamara bought the child from a peasant family as a gift for his wife. You know, like you'd buy a puppy. Others say he picked it from the Sant'Ignazio convent.

Don Trastamara and his wife went on to have their own children, the spitting image of their mother they were, all blond-haired and blue-eyed.'

'What was the first child like?'

Pepe whistled. 'How should I know? I wasn't there. One thing's for sure though, it definitely wasn't blond, because Aunt Suza the seamstress, although she's not really my aunt, she just lives next door to my family, told me she used to go to the estate regularly for dressmaking jobs and she always referred to him as the "the sullen one".'

'The sullen one?'

'Yes, that's right, the sullen one. It means . . .'

'I know what sullen means,' Tomás snapped. He leaned over towards Pepe and grabbed his arm. 'Get up.'

Pepe wriggled out of his grasp. 'What? I'm not going anywhere with you!'

'Don't force me to drag you away,' threatened Tomás. 'I will if I have to.'

The falcon, which had been still during the conversation between the two boys, began to flap its wings in irritation.

Tomás gave it an icy look. 'You are the cause of this disaster, Feather. I cannot allow him to go around revealing my secret. You can do what you want with yours.'

'I won't tell anyone anything, I promise!' exclaimed Pepe, panicking. 'Help me!' he whispered to the falcon. 'Please, don't let him kill me.'

'Oh, for goodness' sake, I'm not going to kill you,' Tomás shouted. 'Just eliminate the threat.'

'Isn't that the same thing?'

'No, not for the moment.'

Tomás yanked Pepe up from the ground, forcing the falcon to abandon its perch. The bird rose into the air and flew after the two figures, the dark-haired boy dragging the deposed king of El Cabanyal in the direction of the dormant fairground.

'Where are you taking me?' asked Pepe, purposely stumbling and dragging his bare feet in an attempt to slow Tomás down.

'Where you won't be able to cause any trouble,' replied the other boy. On arriving at the fair, they went in through one of the side entrances. All the attractions and stalls were closed, although someone was at work with a hammer somewhere.

'This way,' Tomás urged, pushing Pepe between two buildings constructed from a mix of wood and metal, the first being the Haunted House, with strings of skulls and bones hanging around the door, and the other the House of Mirrors, painted purple, yellow and blue. Tomás walked round this one to get to the back where he stopped at a small wooden door, partially hidden behind a barrel. He began fiddling around with the bolt.

'No, wait, don't lock me in there!' Pepe protested. 'Help! Help!'

Tomás gave him a cuff on the head. 'Shut up! Get in quietly or I won't be so nice the next time.'

Meanwhile, the falcon had perched on the barrel and was following the proceedings intently.

Whimpering and whining, Pepe climbed inside the cellar underneath the House of Mirrors.

'Sit tight and don't even think about shouting or screaming for help, otherwise you'll have me to deal with after sunset. Are we understood?'

Pepe chirped meekly in resignation and disappeared inside without further protest.

Tomás slotted the bolt back into place then turned to the falcon. He took Amparo's letter from his pocket and waved it in the air.

'This fire you say you remember, the burning tower,

and . . .' he opened the letter to study the small, neat handwriting, 'the little boy you used to play with. I am not that child,' he stated. 'It can't be me.' He crumpled up the paper and shoved it back into his trouser pocket. He seemed to be about to walk away, but stopped and turned to the falcon.

'I don't have to work tonight. Let's meet here, just before sundown. Okay?'

The falcon beat its wings in agreement and Tomás nodded brusquely, spun around and strode away.

CHAPTER 5

Hours later, when the falcon returned to the fair, the lights were dazzling and people were swarming this way and that, like butterflies flitting from flower to flower, seeking out their preferred attraction. The raptor circled over the House of Mirrors, landed on the wooden barrel concealing the door to Pepe's prison, and waited.

Tomás arrived seconds later, frowning, dark hair tousled, carrying something under his arm. He greeted the falcon with a brief nod and dropped the bundle by the barrel. Amparo's clothes tumbled out.

'The cape looked expensive,' he mumbled by way of explanation.

The falcon clicked its beak as Tomás peeled off his shirt. The olive-skinned torso underneath was marked on the right side of his ribcage by a peculiar dark brown birthmark in the shape of a triangle. 'I rip one every night,' he explained. 'When I'm not working, least I can do is take it off. The seamstresses have enough work without me adding to it. He cleared his throat. 'Can we trust your friend? Do you really think he won't say anything?'

The falcon replied with another click of its beak, Tomás raised his eyebrows slightly, doubtful.

'If you say so . . .' He stared off into space for a second. 'I haven't managed to speak to my adopted mum. She wasn't very lucid today, too much laudanum for the pain. But . . .' he let out a long sigh, 'the truth is, I do remember the flames. And when Pepe mentioned the Trastamara children . . . I remember some pale children with fair hair. Always have. Years ago I even asked Mum if there were other children with me when she found me on the beach, but she always said no. I think I'm beginning to understand where these memories come from. However . . .' he cast the falcon a scowling glance, 'I don't remember you, so don't be getting ideas. Blast!'

The sun had set.

The falcon spread its wings as the long, feathery plumes turned into flesh and bone. The boy kneeled down on the ground, clenching his fists. In the midst of the turmoil, before the transformation was complete, Amparo caught a fleeting glimpse of Tomás's face before it was obscured by the panther's fur and the dark muzzle of the beast replaced his human form.

'Yes, we can trust Pepe!' she whispered hurriedly.

The next second the boy was gone.

Amparo pulled on her clothes to cover up, happy they'd not been lost, and pulled her sage-coloured cape tight around her neck. 'Thank you for this. It was a gift from my grandfather.' She tied the laces on her boots then looked over at the door to Pepe's prison. 'I'm going to let him out, are you okay with that?'

The panther made no objection.

Amparo rifled through Tomás's tattered trousers and found the tiny metal key. She pushed the barrel away and tinkered with the bolt.

'Pepe?' she called into the darkness, on opening the door.

A long silence followed until . . .

'About time!' exclaimed Pepe, emerging from the cellar still tied up in his own shirt. 'I was close to starving to death down there. And I need to pee!'

Amparo rushed to free him. 'I'm sorry.'

'Yeah, I bet,' he muttered. He looked over warily at the panther. 'What have you decided then? To rip me to shreds? Go on, do it. I've been thinking about it all day, you know, and I have put my life in God's good hands. At one point I think he may even have answered me, although you never know with him. But there's really no need to eat me as I am no snitch!'

'We know that, Pepe,' Amparo reassured him.

'Mm,' he grumbled, stretching his arms. 'No one would believe me anyway!'

'True,' Amparo replied quietly. She leaned on the barrel and looked at Pepe. 'Do you want to go home? Your father will be worried.'

Pepe shrugged. 'There's no rush. But before we do anything I need to pee,' he proclaimed with a certain urgency, 'and get a bite to eat.'

The panther emitted a quiet growl and tilted its head to the right. Then it set off, lithe and soundless, leading Amparo and Pepe through the fair and towards his wagon via a series of dark, deserted pathways; hugging the rear of the attractions and skirting any pools of light cast by street lamps.

At the first opportunity, Pepe broke away for a pee, letting loose with a series of colourful exclamations and dubious curses.

Once the three were safely ensconced, alone, inside the wagon, the panther went to lie on the bed while Amparo nodded at some bread lying on a small wooden table by the door.

'May we, Claw?'

The panther whistled, not moving from its spot on the bed.

'I'd take that as a yes,' declared Pepe, already shovelling the bread into his mouth. He looked around, noticing in that moment the drawings pinned to the walls of the wagon. 'I'll say, our panther is quite the artist.'

'He's amazing,' Amparo agreed.

Claw exhaled again and nudged the pillow on the bed with his nose, pushing it on to the floor. Underneath was a slip of paper. The girl picked it up and read the short message on it.

Feather, you're right, we have shared memories. Maybe we can help each other. There could be a reason why, in all these years, my adoptive mum has always refused to bring the Magic Lair to Valencia.

'What do you say, tiger?' Pepe asked, mouth full.

The panther growled. Amparo threw Pepe a warning glare. 'I wouldn't call him tiger if I were you.'

'For heaven's sake, you folk are awful touchy,' Pepe grumbled before chomping down the last hunk of bread. He wiped his hands on his trousers and wrapped the few remaining scraps of his shirt around his neck, scarf-like. 'So are you going to tell me or not?'

Amparo read the note out loud.

'Ah,' commented Pepe. 'You weren't wrong, well done. So what's the plan? Where will we start?'

'Start what?'

'Investigating,' proclaimed Pepe. 'About the panther. Or rather, the boy. The boy and the panther, I mean. Although I can't say I understand what you hope to find out.'

Amparo sat down on the bed beside Claw. 'I believe my past and Tomás's past are connected in some way. See, I know nothing about my parents. They died when I was really young so I always thought I had no memory of them. But when I watched Tomás's magic trick and saw him turn into a panther, something came back to me about my life before I went to live with my grandfather: a fire, a burning tower and a dead child.

'Mm,' Pepe mumbled, lost in thought.

'Seems like he remembers the same things,' continued Amparo. 'More or less.'

'Have you asked your grandfather?' Pepe asked.

'Yes, but he never wants to talk about my parents.'

'Must be a reason why. No doubt about it,' Pepe declared confidently. 'We have a lot of digging, pulling apart and putting back together again to do. Lucky you met me, guys, that was a genuine stroke of luck.'

Amparo raised her eyebrows. 'It was?'

'Oh yes, absolutely. You couldn't pour water out of a boot even if the instructions were on the heel. It's not your fault, it happens when you grown up in the city centre with everything handed to you on a plate.'

'Handed to me on a plate?' Amparo parroted, not knowing whether to laugh or cry or both.

'And this guy here,' Pepe continued, unfazed, pointing to the panther. 'If he is who you think he is, he's not been to Valencia for ten years. What use is that to us? So the plan is, I give you a hand to discover your past, and in return you don't kill me.'

'But we don't want to kill you either way,' Amparo interjected.

'Speak for yourself, I'm not really buying it from this guy,' Pepe interrupted. 'What I'm saying is that you two don't kill me and when we go to the Trastamara estate, because sooner or later that's where we'll go, you'll help me hit up the place for some valuables.'

'Wait, I don't like the sound of this,' Amparo protested. 'I'm not a thief.'

'Neither am I!' Pepe proclaimed vehemently. 'I've never stolen a thing in my life. But it's common knowledge there's still some silverware and other stuff at the estate, of no use to anyone there. So if I take it, I can share it with the people in my neighbourhood who could use it.'

'So why haven't you been out there already to bag some of this treasure?'

'Because they say the estate is haunted,' Pepe revealed. 'Look, it's true, don't laugh. My brother Enrique told me. He went there a few years ago, with Bartomeu and Nofrem, and they came home with faces like soured milk and their tails between their legs. And my brothers are not chicken.'

Amparo and the panther glanced at each other. 'All right,' she replied, reading the glint in the feline's eyes. 'Deal.'

'Good.' Pepe slapped his hands on his knees. 'Now I'm going to go home.'

'What?' Amparo leapt to her feet. 'Aren't we going to do some investigating?'

'At night? With this guy with us?' Pepe retorted, glancing over at the panther. 'We'll go tomorrow morning. You fly so you can hide much more easily, no one will notice you. We can meet at the Torres de Serranos just before lunch. In the meantime, I'll talk to Aunt Suza about the time she worked as a seamstress for the Trastamaras. Maybe we'll find out something else interesting.'

'Why can't we go and talk to Aunt Suza now,' Amparo insisted.

Pepe huffed. 'Well, if it's that important to you, all right,' he conceded. 'We can go now. Maybe she'll have some tortilla left over from yesterday. That bread wasn't enough to feed a sparrow, never mind . . .'

Amparo looked at the panther. 'See you tomorrow, Claw, okay?'

The panther wagged his tail then rested his nose on his paws and turned towards the wall.

'I think he's annoyed,' whispered Amparo, heading for the wagon door. 'Maybe he doesn't want to be left behind.'

'Guys, we need to be rational about this,' Pepe shot back, getting down from the wagon. 'You two are what you are and you only have a half-day each to move around freely. There's not a lot we can do about that.'

'How wise you're getting,' Amparo remarked as they walked away.

'I told you, I've been speaking to God,' said Pepe seriously.

They left the fair with its kaleidoscope of colour and cacophony of sound behind, travelling away from the beach and into the heart of El Cabanyal.

'This way – my father's shop is down here.'

'Weren't we going to see Aunt Suza?'

'She lives right next door.'

Pepe led Amparo through the narrow streets that weaved like a maze through the tapestry of low-rise buildings that were characteristic of El Cabanyal. The girl realised that the neighbourhood wasn't scary at all: each of the two-storey homes was painted a different vibrant colour, showing the diversity and vitality of their inhabitants. Some were well kept with wrought-iron balconies; others had peeling plaster, broken windows, dilapidated doors.

'We're here: Calle de los Ángeles,' Pepe proclaimed proudly when they turned into a long, narrow, bustling road. Half of the street lamps were broken but the inhabitants had decked their windows and ledges with candles and lanterns to make up for it. Dogs criss-crossed the street and a scattering of chickens pecked the ground, oblivious to all the passers-by.

'Pepito,' said the woman sitting in front of the main door. She had a basket of potatoes balancing on her knee and was swiftly and expertly peeling the contents, while a small child, around three years old, was taking the peeled ones and contentedly transferring them to another basket.

'Good evening, Carmen,' Pepe greeted her with a half bow.

The woman cast an inquisitive glance at Amparo then turned to look at Pepe who was quick to reassure his neighbour.

'She's a friend.'

'Ah,' Carmen muttered, with the air of someone who wasn't going to be fooled.

The girl smiled at the woman who didn't return the gesture.

'We don't like strangers here in El Cabanyal,' Pepe whispered. 'Hey, Professor!'

Amparo looked up. Leaning over the balcony of what was probably the smartest, best-kept house in the street was a man in a housecoat, with grey wispy hair and smoking a pipe. Pepe pointed to the intricate white stucco work around the door and windows.

'He did it all himself,' he explained. 'The professor, I mean. He's a real artist.'

'Good evening, Pepe,' the man greeted him. 'Who's your lovely companion?'

'This is Amparo, Professor. We are on a cultural tour around the *barrio*.'

'What a splendid idea, Pepe,' said the man approvingly. 'Keep flying the flag for knowledge, my boy.'

'At your service, Professor, as always.'

Amparo and Pepe kept going, stopping at each building along the way to respond to a greeting or return the regards being offered.

'I've changed my mind,' Amparo said. 'You really are the king of El Cabanyal.'

Filthy, barefoot, wearing a shredded shirt and ripped trousers, Pepe flashed her the biggest smile. In that precise moment, it was like he had everything he could ever want.

'I told you. Oh, here we are at last. Home.' Pepe nodded to the building in front of them and to the right.

It had two storeys like all the others, but the boy's father must've decided the few square metres they provided weren't enough to host his large brood so had added another floor which consisted of a squint-looking attic with a dormer window that was wider than it was high.

'That's where I sleep.' Pepe pointed.

A sizeable group of *barrio*-dwellers had gathered around the shop. Someone had brought out a table and some stools, and a boisterous card game was now taking place by candlelight in the street. A couple of young boys were perched on crates, swinging their feet.

'That's Guillem and Alonso, brothers number five and six,' Pepe explained.

The two boys, whom Amparo could easily have mistaken for twins had she not known they were born a good distance apart, noticed their arrival.

'Father, Pepe's back!' the slightly taller one announced.

From inside the shop, they heard a cacophony of voices, banging and general commotion before a man appeared in the doorway. He was heavyset, ruddy-faced – although most of it was hidden behind a short ginger beard – and his eyes were set close together below thick, expressive eyebrows. A black and yellow striped apron hung over a bulging belly, making him look a bit like a giant hornet.

'Pepe!' he exclaimed, no trace of reprimand in his voice, only genuine relief. 'What a rascal you are . . . you'll be the death of me!

The man came into the street to meet his son, giving him a giant bear hug that lifted the boy almost a metre off the ground.

'What happened to your shirt?'

'It's a long story, Father,' Pepe gasped. 'You're strangling me . . .'

'Oh, sorry, son. Forgive me.'

The man let his son go, then turned his attention to Amparo, who was already being scrutinised by Pepe's brothers. Guillem and Alonso had been joined by another two boys around thirteen or fourteen years old.

'Who's this?' Pepe's father asked, smiling.

'This is my friend Amparo,' Pepe replied.

'Samuel Sorolla,' the man introduced himself, holding out a hand to Amparo.

The girl accepted the hand. 'My pleasure, Don Sorolla.'

Pepe's brothers began snickering and elbowing each other but their father put a very quick stop to it with a threatening glare in their direction.

'Come then, Pepe, let's go inside. It's nearly time for supper.'

'Actually, Father, we have something to do first,' his son objected. 'Have you seen Aunt Suza? Is she home?'

Don Sorolla nodded. 'She got back a few minutes ago. What do you need Aunt Suza for? Even she couldn't save that shirt.'

'It used to be mine,' cackled one of the brothers.

'No, it was mine!' claimed another.

'That shirt has belonged to you all.' Don Sorolla cut them short. 'Well, if you're going to see Aunt Suza, the least you can do is take her something.'

The man disappeared back into the shop only to return a few minutes later with a package wrapped in wax paper.

'We never visit someone's home empty-handed.'

Pepe took the package. 'See you in a bit, Father. Go ahead and start supper without us.'

'You bet we will!' yelled one of the Sorolla brothers as he jumped off his crate.

Pepe gesticulated to him then squeezed Amparo's elbow and nudged her to move. 'Let's go.'

Aunt Suza lived close to the Sorolla house. Her home was a tall, narrow strip of bricks with two windows, one on top of the other, and a weathered wooden door.

Pepe gave the door a vigorous knock. 'Aunt Suza? It's me, Pepe. I brought you a present from my father.'

Amparo tried to peek through a window but the curtain was pulled. The room looked dark inside until a flame suddenly appeared, fluttering around the room then moving towards the door.

The lock clicked and the door opened an inch, just enough to reveal a round and gently wrinkled face, illuminated by a burned-down candle.

'Good evening, Pepe,' said the woman, who was probably around seventy years old. She had short hair – unlike the majority of the women in the Barrio del Carmen who wore their hair in plaits piled into a bun on the top of their heads – and had a pair of small, oval glasses with copper frames.

Pepe handed her the package, which she accepted with a nod of the head.

'Do you want to come in? I have some of yesterday's tortilla left over.'

'It would be a pleasure, Aunt Suza. Can I introduce my friend Amparo?'

'Good evening,' the woman said. She studied the girl for a second then moved away from the door. 'Come in.'

Pepe and Amparo shared a conspiratorial look and went inside.

CHAPTER 6

Aunt Suza beckoned Pepe and Amparo into the tiny kitchen at the back of the house. It overlooked an unevenly shaped garden brightened by a scattering of lemon trees.

The house was furnished sparsely, but it was smart and clean. Amparo sat down at the table with Pepe while Aunt Suza lit another candle – nearly as worn down as the first one – then busied herself with a frying pan.

'Please thank your father for this lovely piece of *jamón*,' the woman said on opening the package Don Sorolla had sent.

'My pleasure, Aunt Suza. My pleasure.'

Amparo was about to speak when Pepe shot her a look full of meaning. They waited for the seamstress to heat up the leftover tortilla, which she served on two vivid azure-blue glazed plates.

'It's delicious,' Amparo mumbled between bites.

The woman sat down opposite the two children. 'Good, I'm glad you like it.' She fixed her glasses with a tap of her index finger and looked at Pepe, curious. 'So tell me, Pepe, what's up?'

'Ah, Aunt Suza,' he began, savouring the last morsel of the omelette, regret flashing in his eyes, 'maybe it's the effect of Las Fallas or something, but folk seem to be going a bit crazy. A couple of nights ago, I got into a bit of a scuffle with that scoundrel Cayetano and he said I'm not a real Sorolla because Dad got me from the foundling wheel at the Sant'Ignazio convent!'

Aunt Suza shook her head. 'That's absurd. I was in the room when you were born.'

'I know, and what with all the children my parents already had, they were hardly going to pick up another random one,' Pepe continued, feigning a level of offence he didn't actually feel. 'Only couples who can't have children go to those kinds of places, not ones that already have seven or eight!' He cackled. 'At best, my folks might've gone there to offload one of my brothers. Alonso, most likely; he's so annoying, worse than a mosquito in your room at night.'

Aunt Suza replied, a note of sadness in her voice, 'I remember a time when the wheel was used almost every day. The sisters barely had time to collect one child before another one arrived.'

'By the way, Aunt Suza,' Pepe whispered furtively, 'is it true what they say about the Trastamaras? That they got a child from the foundling wheel?'

Aunt Suza clicked her tongue. 'Oh, there's been a lot said about the Trastamaras,' she commented. 'Don Ricardo's first son certainly looked nothing like him or his wife. She was from one of those cold northern countries, pale-faced and always poorly. But the children they had later were her spitting image.'

'So what about the first son? Do you think they really got him from the convent?'

Aunt Suza raised her hands. 'Back then, I used to go out to the Trastamara estate regularly, to make dresses for Don Ricardo's wife. And right up until the boy was born, "the sombre one" the servants called him, her measurements never changed.'

Amparo and Pepe shared a knowing look.

'Were there a lot of children on the estate?' Amparo asked. 'Other than the Trastamaras' children, I mean?'

Aunt Suza lay her hands, crossed, on the table and Amparo noticed the marks on her fingers – indentations formed by the needles in her finger joints, the callus on her middle finger, the dry, cracked skin around her nails.

'It would be nice to live somewhere like that,' Pepe commented.

Aunt Suza gave a subdued smile. 'You know what people say, don't you? Appearances are not always what they seem.'

Amparo leaned forward, paying even closer attention. 'What do you mean?'

The old lady's lips pursed and she shook her head gently. 'A prison is still a prison, even if it's lined with gold.'

Amparo wanted to ask more but Pepe threw her a look. 'Thanks for the tortilla, Aunt Suza, it was absolutely divine. And for the chat. We'll let you get to bed now.'

Amparo got up from the table reluctantly and smiled politely at the woman. 'Thank you.'

Aunt Suza gave them a silent nod and accompanied them to the front door.

As the pair stepped outside, the seamstress cleared her throat.

'Back in the day, I used to make monastic clothing, you know, habits and cowls and the like. It didn't pay well, it's something you do out of faith and devotion, and respect for the Mother Superior of the convent.'

'Which convent was that?' Pepe asked.

'Sant'Ignazio,' Aunt Suza concluded, eyes glistening. 'If her tastes haven't changed, she is a great lover of *horchata*, especially the sugary-sweet kind.'

Pepe took the old lady's hands in his and kissed them fervently. 'You're a saint, Aunt Suza! An absolute saint.'

'Let me die first before you canonise me.'

'Ah, but I have a direct line to the Almighty,' Pepe proclaimed, hurrying along the street. 'And he definitely agrees with me!'

Amparo fell in beside him. 'Why didn't you let me ask about the families who lived on the estate?' she whispered.

'She wouldn't have answered,' Pepe replied. 'Not now. She doesn't know you and doesn't trust you. But we learned more than I'd hoped. We just have to wait for tomorrow when we'll go out to the convent with a nice bottle of *horchata*.'

'If only . . .'

Pepe interrupted her. 'We'll visit Aunt Suza again over the next few days if we have to, I promise. And we'll ask about the other children who lived on the estate. Trust me, I know these people. They don't open up readily to strangers.'

'Okay, okay . . .' Amparo conceded.

'Do you want to have dinner at ours?' Pepe offered. 'Dad's in a great mood tonight and Enrique must be out at his girlfriend's. He's so tight-fisted, he is, you'd get nothing to eat if he was on dinner. Dad, on the other hand, he'll have fetched a leg of ham from the attic, mark my word.'

Amparo tried to decline the invitation but Don Sorolla wouldn't take no for an answer. He set up a table with a scattering of stools around it in the street and the entire Sorolla clan sat down as a family, all except the eldest son. Sharing a meal with them around their lively, boisterous and festive dinner table, where everyone argued with everyone yet no one was left with an empty plate, Amparo felt a mixture of joy and sadness. If only her parents hadn't died so young, she thought to herself, she might have had brothers and sisters like Pepe to share the rest of her life with.

The Torres de Serranos stood like ancient sentinels against the expansive canvas of the sea and drifting clouds, their grand arches wide open, watching over the countless passers-by wandering beneath them.

Directly opposite, the Plaza de los Fueros was a hive of activity. Shopkeepers stood in their doorways, ready to welcome or exchange pleasantries with customers. A street trader was standing at the foot of the towers, presenting his wares loudly, while a group of women with baskets over their arms animatedly recounted the details of a recent scandal.

A falcon soared silently above, circled the square, then settled on the sign of a wine shop. Its arrival attracted a number of worried glances until one of the shop owners – a thin man with eyes that bulged like a frog's – emerged into the street and shook his fist at the bird.

'You're scaring my clients, you pest!'

The falcon gave no indication of being bothered by the man's attitude and continued to scrutinise the square.

Its attention was soon captured by the arrival of two boys. One was tall, slim but muscular, with a slightly flattened nose and dark hair that glinted with copper tones in the sunlight. The other was small and scrawny, skinny as a rail, with a bronzed but grimy face and mismatched clothes. Tucked under his arm was a bottle filled with a smooth, creamy liquid.

The two boys stopped in the middle of the square and

looked around. The falcon waited then took flight with a screech. The entire square turned to look, a collective gasp of astonishment rising when the raptor landed on the smaller boy's shoulder.

'What was that you said yesterday?' Tomás asked. 'About Feather being less noticeable than me?'

Pepe, looking a little uncomfortable about the arrival on his shoulder, gave a forced smile. 'You might be right.'

The other boy tutted. 'Shall we go?'

Pepe nodded, keeping the raptor within sight out the corner of his eye. 'Here's hoping she doesn't feel the sudden need to poke me in the eye.'

'Animals never attack for no reason,' Tomás snapped. 'And certainly not for fun. Unlike humans.'

Proceeding a little hesitantly due to the falcon balancing on his shoulder, Pepe led Tomás through the square, around the Torres de Serranos and along the path in the Turia gardens towards the sea. By the time they crossed the ancient Puente de la Trinidad, the scenery had mutated from the thick maze of narrow, winding streets typical of the Barrio del Carmen to the more spacious, quieter feel of the Zaidia neighbourhood.

'It's a long walk to the convent,' Pepe informed them. 'Maybe we can find someone who'll give us a lift. How about you try to smile?' he asked Tomás. 'It would help.'

Tomás ignored him.

They set off along the dusty road that connected Valencia to the farming village of Almassera. The convent was located just before it, on the other side of the Carraixet river.

'How do you know this area so well?' Tomás asked as they made their way in the sun. 'You live by the sea.'

Pepe smiled and tapped his nail on the bottle under his arm. 'My father gets his *horchata* from a supplier in

Almassera. That's how I know the way, and also why I know we'll end up with blisters all over our feet if we don't . . . Ah, look! Hey, *señor*! Excuse me, *señor*!'

A man had appeared on a cart drawn by a mule. He slowed down, albeit a little hesitantly, and looked the boys up and down. When he noticed the falcon he burst out laughing.

'Well, I'll be damned if that's not the queen's falcon!'

Pepe and Tomás exchanged glances.

'I promise, *señor*, we did not steal this falcon from the queen!' Pepe cried. He turned to give the falcon a suspicious look and whispered, 'You don't belong to the queen, do you?'

The man took off his straw hat and wiped the sweat from his forehead with his forearm, laughing. 'Of course you didn't. The queen's falcon is the name of the species, which in full would be *falco eleonorae*, named in honour of Eleonora of Arborea, a Sardinian queen.'

Pepe scratched his head. 'Well, *señor*, I must say, I certainly misjudged you. Who would've thought all the way out here we'd bump into an expert on falcons who even speaks . . . eh, who speaks . . .'

'Latin?' suggested the man.

'Yes, that,' said Pepe, 'right here, in a cloud of dust on the road to Almassera? I certainly didn't.'

'Is that where you're going? Almassera?' the man asked.

'The Sant'Ignazio convent actually,' Pepe specified affably. He showed the man the bottle of *horchata*. 'We have urgent business with the Mother Superior.'

The man glanced at the load in his cart – a dozen shiny oil cans – and shrugged. 'If you can squeeze in there without doing any damage, I can take you as far as the river.'

'Thank you, *señor*!' squealed Pepe, clambering up on to the cart. 'You won't regret it.'

The man waited for Tomás to get in before clicking his tongue and tugging on the reins. The mule brayed loudly and set off, its long ears flapping this way and that to swat away the flies.

'You still haven't told me what you're doing with that falcon,' the man remarked after a bit.

'And you haven't told us how you know so much about falcons,' Tomás fired back.

Pepe grumbled in irritation. 'Do you want to walk? Because I don't, thank you.'

The man didn't seem bothered by Tomás's tone though. 'I used to work with falcons. A long time ago, for a rich gentleman. But I lost my job when he went bankrupt. That's when I started making olive oil with my brother. That's life, eh? Full of surprises.'

'The rich man . . .' Pepe repeated, struck by a sudden thought.

'You won't know him, you would've been a baby when his estate went up in flames. His name was . . .'

'Ricardo Trastamara,' Tomás finished the sentence for him.

The man turned around. 'That's it.' He sat in silence for a few seconds. 'If you know his name, the rumours about him clearly haven't died down yet.'

'The word is that his estate, or what's left of it, is haunted,' Pepe ventured.

'It might have seemed very grand but it was never a happy place,' the man mumbled, more to himself than to the two boys. When the falcon clicked its beak, he turned his attention to the bird.

'What a beautiful bird, young but already well-trained. Did you do that?'

'More or less,' Pepe replied.

'What makes you think,' Tomás interrupted, 'that a

wild animal needs to be trained?'

'Heaven's above, let the saints preserve us,' Pepe exclaimed before throwing Tomás a dirty look. Like before, the man seemed unfussed by the boy's attitude. If anything, he was enjoying it.

'You're not wrong,' he responded, after a moment's reflection.

'I wasn't offering an opinion, merely asking a question.'

'The tone of which made it quite clear what your opinion is,' the man replied. 'To be fair, I couldn't really say. It's human nature, I guess. To control. Contain. Train. It makes us humans feel better.'

'But not the animals.'

'But not the animals,' the man agreed.

The cart trundled along the dusty road. Every now and then a peasant or tradesman travelling in the opposite direction would slow down to exchange a few words or a quick salute with the group, who fell into wide-eyed amazement when they spotted the falcon perched on Pepe's shoulder.

The cart stopped when they got within sight of the Carraixet river.

'That's us, boys. I'm away in the other direction now, to Tavernes Blanques.'

Pepe and Tomás climbed out.

'Thanks for the ride,' said Pepe.

The man tipped his hat in salute then turned the cart north and set off along the trail by the river. Pepe and Tomás lingered for a bit until Pepe slapped a hand to his thigh and pointed to the bridge ahead.

'Let's go, it's not far now.'

The two boys crossed the river and took a path that cut through one empty arid field after another.

'Didn't they grow tiger nut around here? The plant that

stuff there is made of,' Tomás said, pointing to the bottle of *horchata*.

'It's too early yet to plant it,' Pepe explained. 'In about a month or so maybe. Oh, thanks be to God above, there's the convent!'

The building stood on the other side of a piece of fallow land. Within the confines of a tall brick wall, they could still see the whitewashed facade and central bell tower. The surrounding grounds featured an array of small outbuildings, and a heavy wrought-iron gate secured with a chain suggested that uninvited visitors were not welcome.

'Where's this foundling wheel then? I can't see it,' Tomás remarked. 'Are you sure this is the right place?'

'Have faith,' Pepe urged. 'If you're expecting a millstone-size wheel then think again.' He walked along a section of the old brick wall until he came upon a small building that seemed to be part of the wall itself. At its centre was a tiny opening, inside which was a circular wooden contraption with a tiny door.

'This is the wheel,' explained Pepe. 'Open here, put the baby inside, close it, turn the handle and the baby ends up inside the convent.'

Tomás stood in silence, gazing at the unusual mechanism, brows furrowed.

'I don't remember any of this.'

'Well, if you *were* put in here, it's no surprise you don't remember it. You would've been tiny,' Pepe said practically. 'Now let's see if we can get an audience with the Mother Superior.' He raised the bottle of *horchata*. 'This should help.'

They walked back to the gate. Pepe stretched out to reach the bell which hung from one of the stone pillars. He rattled it.

A flock of crows took flight noisily somewhere near

them, upset by the sound. Even the falcon shifted out of discomfort, eventually abandoning Pepe's shoulder to resettle on top of the perimeter wall.

'Doesn't seem to be anyone around,' said Tomás.

'It's a convent. For nuns. Where do you think they might have gone? To eat paella at the seaside? Oh, hello, sister! Good morning!'

A nun had appeared at the main entrance to the convent. She was wearing the traditional black habit, veil and wide white collar with a metal chain around her waist. A set of keys hung from it. It was impossible to say exactly how old she was, but she was definitely fairly long in the tooth, possibly more than eighty.

The old nun approached the gate with a light step.

'Good morning,' she greeted them. 'Are you lost?'

'Not at all, sister, not at all,' Pepe replied. 'This is where we meant to come, specifically to speak with the Mother Superior, if possible.' He held up the bottle. 'We come bearing gifts: *horchata de Almassera*. Syrupy sweet.'

A mischievous look flashed across the old woman's face. 'Can I ask what business you have with the Mother Superior?'

'That, sister, is between me, the Mother and the Lord above,' Pepe said in a hushed tone and with a secretive air. 'No offence intended, clearly, but it's a very private matter.'

'Oh, I understand,' said the nun. 'You boys look hungry,' she added. 'You especially.'

'Well, sister, I never say no to a slice of freshly baked bread, even stale bread either for that matter. When you're being offered Christian charity, one can't be too picky now, can one?'

Tomás mumbled something unintelligible. Pepe ignored him and pointed to the mass of tangled shrubs and hedges on the other side of the gate.

'Sister, what would you say if my friend and I tidied up that sight for sore eyes – no disrespect intended of course – so that we can get it back in full bloom for you in a couple of months? To thank the Mother Superior for the time I know she'll devote to us today.'

The proposal seemed to have hit the right chord with the nun. She took the bunch of keys from her belt, found the one she needed and opened the gate.

Tomás and Pepe walked through and the nun locked the gates behind them again.

'You can make a start on the weeds,' she suggested.

Tomás grumbled to himself, clearly not happy, while Pepe flashed the nun his most dazzling smile.

'Why, thank you, sister. While we do that, can you let the Mother Superior know we're here?'

'Oh, she knows,' the nun replied. 'I'll go and fetch a jug of water and some bread.'

As soon as the nun left the garden, Tomás, who was kneeling over the weeds, shook his head.

'This wasn't part of the plan.'

'We needed a way in,' retorted Pepe. 'If we do this, the Mother Superior will be more willing to help us.'

'Isn't that what the *horchata* was for?'

'You've heard the saying, haven't you? Fortune favours the brave,' Pepe cackled.

Tomás huffed in frustration. The two boys worked in silence for a few minutes, until the sister who had opened the gate to them returned with some bread and water.

'You're making good progress, I see.'

Pepe wiped the sweat from his brow, leaving a grimy streak along his shirtsleeve. 'It's our pleasure, sister. Our pleasure.'

The old lady smiled and placed the snack beside the shrubs. 'The Mother Superior will receive you shortly.

When you're finished with those weeds, come inside and up the stairs. On the first floor you'll see a wooden door with an angel carved on the left side.'

'Thank you, sister,' said Pepe. 'We'll leave you to your prayers, now.'

The nun nodded and went back inside the convent. Pepe resumed his work with renewed vigour and, in a matter of minutes, had pulled all remaining weeds from around the shrubs. He drank a couple of glasses of water and tore the loaf of bread in two, handing one half to Tomás.

'Do you want it?'

Tomás shook his head and Pepe was more than happy to accept a second ration.

'Things always seem clearer on a full stomach,' he commented, finishing his snack. He turned to the falcon who was still sitting on the perimeter wall. 'See you in a bit.'

Inside the convent was cool and silent, the air imbued with the mild scent of incense. Through an archway they could see a porticoed courtyard with a water fountain gurgling quietly in the centre. A middle-aged man whose clothes were hidden behind a long brown apron was brushing dust and leaves from one of the paths into the grass.

'This way,' Tomás indicated. 'The nun said we're to go upstairs.'

The two boys climbed the stone steps to the first floor. They recognised the room they were to meet the Mother Superior in straight away, from the description they'd been given of the door.

Tomás knocked vigourously.

'Come in,' a voice summoned from inside.

Tomás pressed down on the bronze door handle and stepped in to the room, Pepe on his heels. It was a large room, sparsely furnished, walls painted grey and the stations of the cross hanging on both sides.

They couldn't see the Mother Superior's face initially because she was cast in silhouette on a high-backed chair behind an imposing, solid wood desk. They stepped in a little closer.

The Mother Superior smiled. 'I hope you'll forgive me.'

'Oh, of course, Mother Superior.' Pepe reached the desk and set down the bottle of *horchata*. 'This is for you.'

The nun looked at the bottle and sighed. 'Are my bad habits really that well known to have travelled beyond these walls?'

'Oh, *horchata*'s not a bad habit, Mother!' Pepe cried earnestly. 'Let's say it's – how can I put it – a way of supporting the local economy. Moreover, it was a woman who knows you well who told me about the *horchata*. Aunt Suza. The seamstress.'

'Ah, Suza. I haven't seen her in ages. How is she?'

'Well,' replied Pepe. 'The biggest chatterbox ever. When she chooses, that is.'

Tomás cleared his throat, growing impatient.

The nun turned her attention to him. 'Tell me why you're here.'

'We're here to ask about a child left in the foundling wheel around fourteen years ago,' Tomás rushed to explain.

The nun remained impassive before the request. 'Very many children were left with us in that period. One a day, I believe, possibly more. There's no way I can remember them all.'

'You'd remember this, surely, if you'd seen it before,' replied Tomás, lifting up his shirt to reveal the dark birthmark on his side. 'It's a very unusual shape.'

The Mother Superior sat, eyes half closed, absorbed in her thoughts.

'Might I remind you that lying is a sin.'

'Tomás!' Pepe scolded. 'Forgive him, Mother, he's not used to . . .'

The Mother Superior raised a hand and Pepe fell silent. 'No. Your friend is right. Lying is a sin. What he says is true. I saw that mark many years ago, maybe fourteen as you say, on a newborn only a few weeks old that was left in the wheel. If you want to know who left the child though, that I can't tell you.'

'But can you tell us who adopted it?' Tomás asked, lowering his shirt.

'Yes,' she replied, a faint, sad smile crossing her lips. 'It was the only time I ever regretted a decision I took.'

'What decision?' asked Tomás.

'Two families wanted you,' explained Mother Superior. 'The first was a modest one, a couple who ran a shop, advanced in years. The second family was rich and powerful. I made the wrong decision – I rushed into it. I needed money to feed all the young mouths we were caring for in those days. Money the first family did not have.'

'But the second one did?' Tomás deduced.

'They were very generous. Too generous to turn down.'

'You're talking about the . . .' Tomás began.

'The Trastamaras,' the Mother Superior concluded. 'I could never have known what a ruinous end they would come to. Why didn't you go with her when the estate went up in flames and the wife fled with the children?'

'I don't know,' replied Tomás. 'I have no memory of the fire.' He shrugged. 'Maybe she chose to leave me behind. After all, I wasn't her real son.'

A long silence followed, both Tomás and the Mother Superior engulfed by dark thoughts and filled with regret.

Pepe cleared his throat. 'Forgive me, Mother Superior,

but did Tomás not have anything with him from his birth family at all?'

'No. I'm sorry. He was wrapped in a simple cloth like all the others.'

'Do you still have it?' Tomás immediately asked.

The Mother Superior shook her head again. 'No, I'm sorry.'

'Okay, I understand.' Tomás turned and hurried out the room, not leaving the nun time to say anything else.

'Please excuse him,' said Pepe. 'He was hoping to find answers coming here.'

The nun nodded, sad. 'There are times when it's better not to know.'

'Is this one of those times?'

The Mother Superior did not reply, and Pepe sensed the conversation was over.

'Thank you for your time, Mother Superior. Good day.'

The young boy left the room in silence, feeling the nun's eyes on his back and the belief in his heart that if she'd been able, she would've told him more. A lot more.

CHAPTER 7

When Pepe made it outside the convent, he found Tomás by the perimeter wall with a stern-looking nun who was fussing with the chain around the gate. The falcon hadn't moved from its perch and was following the scene intently.

After some muttering, the nun finally managed to get the padlock open. 'Right, off you go now,' she instructed the boys.

Tomás marched out without giving her a second glance, while Pepe tipped his head in respect. The nun ignored them both.

'Listen,' began Pepe, but Tomás was hurrying along the road without him.

'What an absolute waste of time,' he exploded.

The falcon flew down from the wall and returned to its perch on Pepe's shoulder, making him jump.

'I don't think I'll ever get used to this . . . Tomás, wait!'

Tomás spun around. 'Why should I wait? I've just been told that I was abandoned as a newborn in the foundling wheel of a convent then the woman who was supposed to care for me like a mother left me to die in the flames of a raging fire!'

'We don't know what really happened that night,' said Pepe.

Tomás shook his head. 'I should never have gotten involved in this. It's all your fault, Feather!' he cried in anger, pointing a finger at the falcon which squawked and spread its wings abruptly, hitting Pepe in the eye.

'Would you two rein it in!' he shouted. 'For crying out loud, that hurt.' Pepe groaned and rubbed his face. 'Listen, getting angry doesn't do anyone any good. I can't force you to keep digging into your past,' he said, addressing Tomás. 'If you don't want to know then why on earth should I? But if you stick with it, I think we could find out a lot more.'

'I've found out more than enough already.'

'I disagree.'

Tomás shook his head. 'So how exactly do you plan to find out *a lot more*?' he snapped, emphasising the last three words.

'Didn't you see what was on the Mother Superior's desk?'

'A bunch of stuff,' Tomás retorted.

'Letters,' Pepe clarified. 'Letters and sealed envelopes ready to be delivered.'

'And why is that of any interest to us?'

'If I'm right, you'll see why.'

Tomás followed Pepe reluctantly. The two of them crossed the road to wait on the other side.

They didn't have long to wait. Around ten minutes later, the man who'd been sweeping the courtyard only half an hour earlier stepped out of the convent with a satchel over his shoulder. He set off along the road at a brisk pace, heading in the opposite direction from where Tomás and Pepe had arrived.

'Let's follow him,' Pepe said.

Tomás put up no resistance, despite the sceptical look on his face.

The road was lined with tangles of bramble bushes and tall cypress trees. The two boys ducked into impromptu hiding places along the way as best they could and the only reason they weren't spotted was because the man had no reason to think he might be being followed. A little later they reached a house. It was a modest stone and brick construction with dark roof tiles. Encircling it was a vast, bare expanse of earth that would soon be transformed into fields of tiger nuts.

The man left the main road, taking the path that led to the house. He knocked on the door. The door opened and a woman appeared in the doorway holding a small baby. Another two children were holding on to her skirt. She and the man began to speak.

'We're too far away to hear anything,' muttered Tomás.

'I'm not interested in what they're saying, I just want to see what's in his bag,' Pepe replied.

'Why?'

'You'll see.'

The man had just opened the bag and was rummaging around inside it. Losing his patience, he eventually pulled out a handful of envelopes and flicked through them. He handed one to the woman along with a small bundle.

Pepe was elated. 'I was right! He's delivering the convent's post.'

'Do you think the Mother Superior is warning people of our visit?'

'I don't think she told us the whole truth,' Pepe declared, thinking back to the nun's closing words.

Tomás, deep in thought, watched the man take his leave of the woman.

'Do you want to rob him?'

'Well, erm, yes.'

'How do we get his bag without him seeing us?'

Pepe eyed the falcon with a satisfied smile. 'I think I might have an idea.'

Manuela
(Conselle Vega Fince d'Alven)

As the man ran away screaming, the falcon flying after him, Pepe dived over to the bag that had fallen to the ground and tipped out the contents.

'Quick, let's have a gander at these before he comes back,' he urged, rifling through the envelopes and small packages wrapped in fabric. A pair of baby socks slipped out of one. Tomás picked them up and put the package back together carefully, securing it with the string that had come lose. Pepe, meanwhile, was scanning the envelopes, one by one.

'Do any of these names mean anything to you?' he asked, handing them to Tomás who accepted them a little unwillingly.

'Don Anacleto, Donna Blanca, Famiglia Gutierrez . . .' Tomás shrugged his shoulders. 'Nope, nothing at all.' He picked up all the letters and parcels the nuns had made up for the needy and returned them to the satchel. 'Let's get out of here.'

'Wait, wait,' Pepe mumbled, 'what did you say the woman who raised you is called?'

'Manuela. Why?'

Pepe handed Tomás one of the final letters. He took it and flipped it over. On the back, in the smallest, neatest handwriting were a few unmistakable words:

Manuela
(Magic Lair, Valencia Fair)

CHAPTER 8

By the time they made it back to the fair, a lot of the attractions were already open, and crowds of fairgoers had begun to gather around the stalls and tents. Tomás and Pepe, with the falcon following them from above, headed towards the Magic Lair which, according to the sign at the entrance, for the first time ever in Spain, would be staging the finest tricks from the distant and mysterious lands of the Orient.

'Looks interesting,' Pepe remarked.

Tomás gave a half growl in response. Pepe sighed.

'Don't rush to conclusions Tomás. Maybe your mother will have an explanation.'

Tomás skirted the Magic Lair tent.

'The letter spoke loud and clear,' he replied. 'She has always known who I am.'

'Well, no, not really, that's not what it said.'

Tomás showed no sign of acknowledging Pepe's objection. They walked in silence to the wagon park, which was quiet and deserted, and headed for Donna Manuela's wagon. Hers was one of the smallest, but it appeared to be well kept on the outside, painted a soft blue, with the wheels a more vibrant orange. Tomás climbed the few wooden steps and knocked on the door.

'Mum? I need to speak to you.'

A feeble 'come in' could be heard from inside.

Tomás turned the handle but before going in, glanced up at the falcon, which had perched on the roof of a nearby wagon, and down at Pepe, who was standing at the bottom of the steps.

'I think I should wait for you here, outside,' suggested Pepe.

'No,' replied Tomás, to Pepe's surprise. 'It's thanks to you I know what happened. Come with me.'

'To be fair, it's actually thanks to Amparo, even though you had a go at her earlier.'

Tomás looked at the bird. 'Sorry, Feather. Pepe's right.'

The falcon left its perch and flew over to Donna Manuela's wagon, where it settled on the window ledge.

Tomás threw open the door and Pepe, dragging his feet slightly, climbed the steps after him. Inside, the wagon was clean and tidy. Most of the space was taken up by a wooden bed, the frame of which was painted blue and orange, to match the exterior. Unlike Tomás's wagon though, the walls were bare, the only exception being an unsettling portrait of a young man. Or at least Pepe assumed he was young, going by the meticulously defined contours of the face and the dark, flowing hair, while the eyes, nose and mouth were barely sketched, veiled by a smoky aura that made it impossible to discern the man's true features.

'Tomás,' Donna Manuela called out. Pepe turned his attention to the woman lying on the bed. He figured she couldn't be any older than sixty, sixty-five, but the illness she was suffering from, whatever it was, seemed to have aged her. She was gaunt, with a delicate pallor so translucent that not even the sun's rays would be able to restore some colour to it. Large hazel eyes contrasted with the white streaks in her brown hair.

She must've been beautiful as a young woman.

Tomás approached the bed. 'How are you today?'

'Better,' she replied, which was clearly a lie. She shifted her gaze to Pepe, who was standing awkwardly by the door. 'Is this a friend of yours?'

'You could say,' Tomás replied.

'My name is Pepe,' Pepe introduced himself. 'Pleased to meet you.'

Donna Manuela smiled while Tomás sat down on the bed and took one of his mother's hands in his. 'I need to ask you something and I want the truth.'

Donna Manuela looked at her adopted son with a mixture of fatigue, fear and resignation. 'You know, don't you? I feared that coming back here would be a mistake, but the fair committee gave me no choice, their minds were made up. I managed to keep us all away from this city for years, but they wouldn't hear of it this year, and we need the money. We couldn't stay in Barcelona alone.'

She coughed and Tomás picked up the jug on her bedside table and and splashed some water into a glass for her. Donna Manuela sipped it slowly then, unsteadily, put the glass down.

'You didn't find me on the beach in Barcelona when I was a child, did you?' Tomás began.

'No, I didn't. I saved you from the fire. Here, in Valencia.'

'At the Trastamara estate.'

Donna Manuela nodded.

'But Don Ricardo Trastamara and his wife are not my real parents. I am not their son.'

'No, you're not.'

'So whose son am I?'

'I don't know,' Donna Manuela replied straight away. 'Please believe me, Tomás, when I say I don't know.'

Tomás delved into his pocket and pulled out the note

the Mother Superior had addressed to her. He opened it and read it aloud.

'*E.G. is back. Take the boy away.*' Tomás glanced at his mother whose eyes were now vacant. It's signed P. It was sent by . . .'

'The Mother Superior of the Sant'Ignazio convent,' Donna Manuela concluded. 'Her name is Pilar.'

Tomás pursed his lips. 'Who's E.G.?'

'E.G. is the reason I made sure you never returned to Valencia in all these years, even though I knew it meant denying you the chance to reconstruct your past.' She stopped and stared vacantly into her embroidered bedcover for a second. 'The truth is, I have the desperation and unhappiness of so many families on my conscience. So many disappeared children. And it's all my fault.'

'Mother, I don't understand. What disappeared children?'

Donna Manuela shook her head, her hair swaying gently in the air. 'It's a long story. Long and complicated.'

'Don't I deserve to hear it, if it has something to do with me?'

Donna Manuela nodded. 'Yes, you deserve to know.' She cleared her throat then began to recount her tale. 'I was born in a small village at the foot of Mount Puig Campana, not far from Alicante, in 1855. My family led a simple life but we were happy. We had some land that we farmed and some livestock. My mum was a good cook so she helped out occasionally at the local inn and would often bring treats home for my brother and me: fresh bread, fruit and, when we were really lucky, even some cake. Like I said, we were happy with the simple things.'

Donna Manuela stopped to catch her breath. Her voice was low and gravelly, hypnotically so, and Pepe found himself mesmerised by the story and eager to hear more.

'Our neighbours were richer than us, the father ran a

small shop selling fabrics, they had one child, but I've never met a sadder family than them. The parents had fallen out of love very early on and the child had paid the price. Maybe it was out of pity, initially anyway, but I made friends with him. Over time though, I learned what a sensitive child he was. Julio – that was his name – had a good heart, he was always ready to help others, and I grew to truly enjoy his company. However, as he got older, he started to change. He became obsessed with the idea of getting rich, said that as soon as he was old enough, he'd move to Madrid to seek his fortune, that he'd open multiple shops and become a man of importance. Sadly, when he eventually reached that age, he realised he couldn't afford to leave. So he stayed and helped his father sell fabric but his frustration grew and grew. Despite all this, my feelings for him never changed, if anything they became stronger. I knew that the sweet, sensitive child I'd made friends with was still in there somewhere. Until one day when everything changed.'

Enthralled by the story, Pepe had moved closer to the women and, without realising it, was now perched on the end of her bed.

'Everyone who lived at the foot of Mount Puig Campana had heard of a village that had once existed on the northern ridge and of which only a few ruins remained,' Donna Manuela continued. 'All the children believed it was cursed, haunted by ghosts and inhabited by a monster, which, several decades earlier, had scared all the inhabitants of the village away. We teenagers thought it was just a sad, desolate place, even if none of us had ever been brave enough to go there. One day in May, however, Julio had a violent argument with his father about work and he asked to me come out for a walk with him so he could let off some steam.

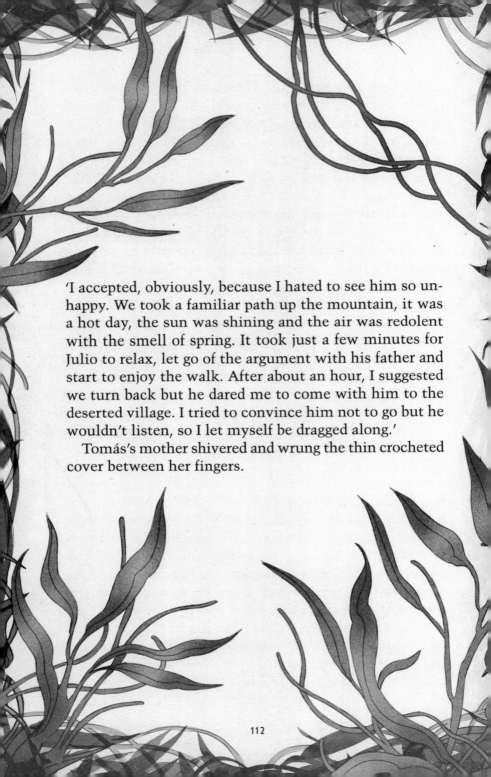

'I accepted, obviously, because I hated to see him so un-
happy. We took a familiar path up the mountain, it was
a hot day, the sun was shining and the air was redolent
with the smell of spring. It took just a few minutes for
Julio to relax, let go of the argument with his father and
start to enjoy the walk. After about an hour, I suggested
we turn back but he dared me to come with him to the
deserted village. I tried to convince him not to go but he
wouldn't listen, so I let myself be dragged along.'

Tomás's mother shivered and wrung the thin crocheted
cover between her fingers.

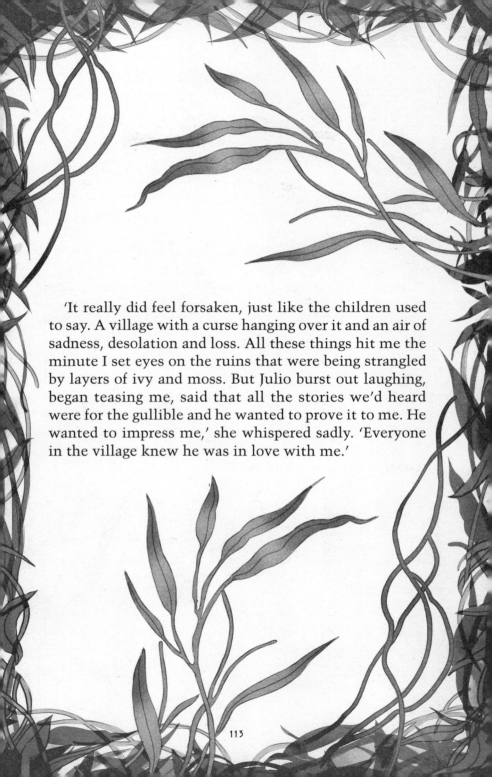

'It really did feel forsaken, just like the children used to say. A village with a curse hanging over it and an air of sadness, desolation and loss. All these things hit me the minute I set eyes on the ruins that were being strangled by layers of ivy and moss. But Julio burst out laughing, began teasing me, said that all the stories we'd heard were for the gullible and he wanted to prove it to me. He wanted to impress me,' she whispered sadly. 'Everyone in the village knew he was in love with me.'

'And were you in love with him?' Pepe couldn't help asking. 'Were you?'

Donna Manuela smiled. 'Oh yes. I'd learned to see the goodness in Julio and to forget all the rest, something everyone else seemed unable to.'

'So what happened?' Tomás interjected impatiently.

Donna Manuela shook her head. 'I didn't go after him. I stayed where I was, on the outskirts of the village, while he set off along the path and disappeared around a bend.'

Pepe gripped the edge of the bed. 'And then?' he murmured, almost inaudibly.

'He was euphoric when he came back: laughing hysterically and holding a heavy gold key in his hand. He said his problems were over, that thanks to the gold he'd be able to leave the village he hated and move to the capital. He asked me to go with him but I wanted to know, first, where he'd got the gold key from, if he'd stolen it from a grave. He swore he hadn't, and I wanted to believe him.

'We made our way home and went our separate ways for the night. The idea of going to Madrid with him – we'd have to marry first, obviously – excited me. I was happy with my family but I knew I'd need to find a husband sooner or later and build my own family. I lay awake all night, thinking of the answer I'd give Julio the next morning. When dawn finally broke . . .'

Tomás groaned in impatience, Pepe imagined he probably didn't understand what all this story between his adoptive mother and her fiancé, or her would-be fiancé, had to do with him. Pepe was also struggling to see the connection, yet he still found it made incredible listening.

'I went to Julio's house. His mother was at the market with mine, his father had gone to Alicante to collect a batch of fabric. I hoped that meant we'd be able to speak in peace, about our plans. When I knocked, however, Julio

wouldn't open the door. He even tried to send me packing, shouting and throwing things at the door. I didn't give up, I went round the back, climbed over the wall and got in through the kitchen, just like I'd done all the time when we were little. He was there, inside, kneeling down, holding his face in his hands, a face that was no longer his.'

'What do you mean?' Tomás asked. 'Had he transformed too? The same thing that happens to me?'

Donna Manuela shook her head. 'No, what happened to Julio was nothing like you, but . . . it was no longer him. The look in his eyes was evil, like a beast about to pounce on its prey. His features – he'd always been handsome, the most handsome boy in the village – had turned chiselled and hard. I was afraid just to look at him. In fact, I screamed and backed away, disgusted. He tried to stop me but I ran away. That was the last time I ever saw him.'

'Why?' asked Tomás.

'Because he left. He left our village that same day, and no one heard from him again. Not as Julio Alameda, that is.'

Tomás looked down at the note he was holding. '*E.G. is back*,' he read.

'El Gris,' Donna Manuela finally revealed. 'The Grey One.'

'So who's that then?' asked Tomás, visibly irritated. 'Why do I have to leave Valencia because he's back? Back from where? From prison?'

Donna Manuela seemed to shrink before the questions Tomás fired at her. 'El Gris steals children like you, Tomás. No one knows why nor what he does with them, but none of them have ever returned.'

'Children like me?' echoed Tomás. 'Are there a lot of us then?'

Donna Manuela nodded. 'So it would seem.'

'Why did you say you have the burden of the disappearance of all these children on your conscience?' Pepe interrupted. 'What does this El Gris have to do with you?'

'I think El Gris and Julio are one and the same. And if I hadn't rejected him that morning because of how he looked, those children would not have disappeared into thin air.'

A long silence followed, which Pepe eventually broke.

'Donna Manuela, please excuse me, what you are saying doesn't make sense. You didn't kidnap those children, that man did, whoever he was.'

'Why did the Mother Superior write to you? What does she know?' Tomás pressed her for answers.

'Pilar is from the same village as Julio and I originally. When he and I were born, just a few months apart, Pilar had just taken her vows and ran the local school. She noticed what a state I was in and how distraught I was at Julio's disappearance, so I confided in her. She listened and consoled me as best she could. Time went by, Pilar continued doing her charity work and was soon well known, even outside our province. One day, years after the events I've just described, she came to see me, just as she was preparing to move to Valencia, to the Sant'Ignazio convent. I'd never married, not that I hadn't had my share of proposals, so she suggested I go with her. I knew a nun's life wasn't for me, so I politely declined. Before she said goodbye, Pilar told me she'd heard rumours about a man who kidnapped "different" children. She didn't go into detail, but I knew immediately who she was referring to.'

'Have you never asked her more about this?' urged Tomás, voice trembling in both accusation and disbelief.

Donna Manuela's reply was a look of absolute shame, and Pepe felt a stab of sympathy that was quite unusual for him.

'*Different children*,' mumbled Tomás, glancing at the falcon outside the window.

Donna Manuela nodded. 'People didn't understand, initially, why some children were disappearing and others weren't. So Pilar began asking around, speaking to families, investigating. Most wouldn't speak initially, you can imagine – they were scared what people would think, not just their neighbours but also the Church: to be accused of witchcraft or worse. But Pilar has never been one to give up and she eventually discovered that all the children who'd disappeared shared one trait.'

'Did they only disappear in this area?' Pepe asked.

'No, also in Alicante, Sagunto, Alzira, Barcelona . . .'

'Do you think the Mother Superior knows who I am?' interrupted Tomás. 'And who my parents are? Is there some reason she doesn't want to tell me?'

Donna Manuela shook her head. 'If Pilar says she doesn't know, then she doesn't know.'

'And what were you doing at the Trastamaras' the night of the fire?' Tomás's tone betrayed levels of anxiety and impatience that were on the verge of bubbling over into anger, which Pepe could understand to a degree. Donna Manuela had filled their heads with information but none of what she'd said was of any use to Tomás in finding his biological parents.

'I . . .'

Donna Manuela flopped back on her pillows, as if the physical and emotional toll from the long and gruelling conversation had brought her to breaking point. Beads of sweat had formed all over her pale face and she was gasping for air.

'Oh no!' Tomás rushed to pour her a glass of water and held it up to her mouth, but the woman was shaking so violently she couldn't even manage a sip. The boy turned to Pepe.

'Go and get Ester, the herbalist. She's in the wagon next to this one. She'll know what to do. Be strong, Mother,' he whispered gently. 'Everything will be all right.'

Pepe dashed out of the wagon and banged on the one next door. 'Open up, please, Donna Manuela is sick!'

The door flew open and a woman, dressed in black from

head to toe, appeared in the doorway. Ester was much younger than Donna Manuela and had a beautiful mane of long honey-coloured hair, all the way down to her waist, and large green eyes. Pepe had never seen such a beautiful woman before and found himself staring, mouth hanging open.

'*Què has dit?*' she asked in Catalan.

Pepe recovered from his surprise and pointed to the wagon next door. 'Donna Manuela! She has taken ill!'

Ester muttered a series of words that were incomprehensible to Pepe, then went back inside her wagon. She re-emerged a few seconds later carrying a small medical bag with glass vials, bandages and medical instruments poking out. They rushed to Donna Manuela's wagon, went inside and Pepe heard her debating animatedly with Tomás, who reappeared in the doorway when quiet had fallen once again in the wagon.

Still gripping Mother Superior's letter in his hand, Tomás descended the wooden steps, head hanging down. He looked at Pepe distractedly.

'I'd like to be alone.'

The falcon left the window ledge and flew back to Pepe's shoulder.

'Are you sure?' queried Pepe.

Tomás nodded and shuffled away, leaving the wagon park and disappearing into the crowds of strangers milling around in search of thrills and excitement.

CHAPTER 9

'You look worried. Is anything wrong?'

Amparo was sitting at the dinner table with her grandfather, picking at a slice of bread, her mind elsewhere but with no desire to give voice to her thoughts. She knew that to express them would only lead to a pointless argument. Mariano had already made it clear he did not want to talk about his granddaughter's parents or how they had died. *Maybe he's not lying*, Amparo thought to herself. Maybe her parents really had died at sea. But meeting Tomás had triggered memories of things that had been pushed into the darkest corners of her mind, things she needed to make sense of if she were ever to find peace.

'I'm just a bit tired,' Amparo replied. 'Can I go to bed?'

Mariano looked at his granddaughter, perplexed, and took a long puff on his pipe. 'Of course. I'll clear up this evening, if you want. Then I have a piece to finish for Las Fallas in my workshop; they're setting up the sculptures tomorrow. That's where you'll find me if you need me.'

Amparo nodded and hurried up the stairs to her bedroom.

She lay down on the bed, shut her eyes and tried to make sense of all the ideas racing around her head.

Her head refused to cooperate though, and a barrage of confusing, disconnected images continued to swirl around. Instead of trying to grasp them, she decided to let them flow freely, to dance and spin like leaves caught in a sudden gust of wind.

The smell of burning and the glow of red. Concern in the voices of adults – maybe her parents? Amparo in a small, dark place, but not afraid, quite the opposite; she feels safe. At home. The door swings suddenly open and someone – something – comes in, banging into the kitchen table. The noise of plates crashing to the floor. An animal . . . a cat maybe? No, it's too big. Amparo runs towards it and finds herself looking into a black muzzle bathed in the glow of two large green eyes.

'Claw,' Amparo mumbled, springing up. 'I lived with the Trastamaras too!'

The doubt that had been gnawing away at her for days had become a certainty. She and Tomás had a shared past.

She lay back down on her side and hugged her knees.

Pepe was right, we need to go to the estate.

She closed her eyes, worn out from the events of the day and all the things they'd discovered. She had no idea where Tomás was now or what he was doing as a panther, she only hoped it wasn't anything silly. The look on his face when Donna Manuela had told them the story of El Gris and his connection to the missing children had belied the anger, frustration and deep sadness he was feeling. Amparo wondered if Tomás had ever felt happy and the thought of it gave her a knot in the stomach.

She pulled the covers up around her neck and waited for sleep to help her find a peaceful escape from the day's troubles.

The next day, a young, barefoot boy never seen before in the Barrio del Carmen came asking around for 'the carpenter working on the *falla* sculpture' and his granddaughter. People in the neighbourhood were initially suspicious of the sly-looking boy and ignored him. That was until Don Sebastià's giant dog bounded over to him, wagged his tail and gave the boy a long lick on the face.

'Hello, gorgeous boy. You remember me, don't you?'

Don Sebastià had been out for a stroll. He approached the stranger. 'Are you the one looking for Mariano and his granddaughter Amparo?'

'That's me indeed, *señor*. You have my word though – I am not here to make trouble.'

Don Sebastià laughed. 'I guessed that.' He glanced down at Pepe's bare feet. 'What happened to your shoes?'

'Ah, last week I got into a bit of a scuffle with three of my brothers – Pere, Guillem and Alonso. Three against one, call that fair? A bunch of clucking great chickens they are, hiding behind each other like that! You wouldn't believe it, *señor*, how they robbed me. Made off with my shoes, they did, but with the thrashing I gave them, they'll not be laying hands on me anytime soon!'

Taken aback by the torrent of words and the fervour with which they were delivered, all Don Sebastià could do was ask, 'What's your name?'

'Pepe Sorolla, *señor*. At your service.'

'Come with me, young man. I have a pair of my son's old shoes I can give you. I live across the street from Mariano and his granddaughter. Just down there, see? The door next to that beggar sitting on the ground.'

Pepe nodded. 'Your word is my command, my kind

benefactor.'

'Aren't you the talker,' remarked Don Sebastià, shaking his head. 'Do you go to school?'

'School? Absolutely not,' Pepe replied. 'My education is in the very capable hands of the famous professor, Tiberio Bennássar Marin, in El Cabanyal. Have you heard of him? He taught at the university when he was young. The man's a genius, I tell you. A genius and an artist, you mark my word.'

'That I will,' Don Sebastià stated, half amused and half in awe of the young boy who was nothing but skin and bone but so full of life. 'Here we are.' The man opened the front door as the corpulent beggar muttered a confused greeting before dozing off again. 'You wait here, I won't be a minute.' Don Sebastià disappeared inside, leaving Pepe in the street with Tiano, who was now licking the boy's shins like they were a pair of tasty chicken drumsticks. When his master reappeared carrying two sturdy leather shoes, the dog was still fully absorbed in his exploration of the boy's legs.

'Tiano, leave the boy alone! They'll be nothing left of him! Here, try these on. They may be a bit big, but nothing a thick pair of socks can't fix.'

Pepe's face lit up and he flashed the man an enormous grin as he accepted the shoes. He put them on and thanked Don Sebastià profusely, despite the shoes being visibly enormous on his feet. 'My brothers will be so jealous!' he concluded.

Don Sebastià cackled and pointed at the door across the road. 'That's where Mariano and Amparo live. I think he's in his workshop and Amparo is resting. She doesn't keep well, the poor girl. The sun bothers her. I haven't seen her since last night.'

Pepe pulled a piece of paper out of the only intact pocket

in his trousers. 'I just need to leave her this.'

'Slip it under the door,' Don Sebastià suggested. 'I'd say give it to me but Tiano eats anything he can get his teeth around. I wouldn't like it to end up in his stomach.'

Pepe took the man's advice and slipped the note under the door. He thanked Don Sebastià again for the shoes and skipped away down the road, the heels of his new shoes clicking cheerfully on the cobbles.

When Mariano arrived home hours later with the falcon on his shoulder, he spotted the note on the floor straight away, the name Amparo marked in wobbly letters on the front.

The falcon left its perch and flew upstairs. Half an hour later, when the sun had dipped out of view on the horizon and night had fallen, Amparo ran downstairs and glanced over at the door. The note was still there, on the floor.

'As you can see, I haven't touched it,' Mariano commented from over by the sink where he was slicing onions. 'It has your name on it, not mine.'

Amparo picked it up and opened it. She read the few words hatched in Pepe's wobbly handwriting then slipped the note into her dress pocket.

'Can I go out?'

Mariano finished chopping the onions and tipped them into an old, chipped bowl. 'What about dinner?'

'I'll get something out,' she replied. 'There's a churros cart at the corner of Calle de San Ramon,' she suddenly recalled. 'I'd like to go there and have a look at the stalls.'

'With the person who sent you the note?' Mariano asked.

Amparo nodded.

Mariano gave his approval with a deep sigh. 'Okay, go. But don't be late back. The offering of flowers started yesterday in Plaza de la Virgen and it's like the entire province is milling around the city. Be careful.'

Amparo took her sage cape from the hook by the door. 'Okay. I'll not be long, I promise.'

Mariano smiled. 'See you later.'

The girl left the house. The *falla* representing the Barrio del Carmen had finally been erected and the neighbourhood was buzzing with people from other parts of city who had come to see the giant sculpture for themselves. Amparo realised there was only one day to go until the night of 19th March when all the *fallas* across Valencia would be set alight, with the exception of the winning ones. This would normally fill her with excitement and enthusiasm, but her mind was elsewhere this year.

She greeted Don Sebastià, who was sitting on his usual wooden chair, Tiano at his feet, intent on observing the crowds and sharing a few words with the odd passer-by. Amparo noticed an empty space where the bulky silhouette of the beggar was normally stationed. She gave this no more than a distracted thought, presuming that, after so many years, he'd finally moved on to another part of the city.

Elbowing her way through the crowds, she reached Calle Caballeros first, then Plaza de la Virgen where the giant wooden statue of the Virgin Mary was covered, almost head to toe, in flowers. A heady, floral scent hung over the square, melding with the equally fragrant smell of fried churros rising from the stalls.

Amparo cut across the square, walked past El Micalet, the cathedral bell tower, and entered the narrow Calle de la Barchilla. Pepe was waiting for her there, under the archway of the same name. He smiled when he saw her coming and lifted a foot in the air. 'Look what I've got. Aren't they amazing? Your neighbour, the man with the dog, he gave me them.'

Amparo noticed the shoes were at least two sizes too big and that Pepe had tried to remedy the situation with a thick pair of knee-length socks.

'They look great,' she conceded. 'Where's Claw?'

'Well, I could hardly come into the city with a panther in tow, could I?' retorted Pepe. 'He's waiting across the river. I've also managed to procure us a cart and mule to get out to the Trastamara estate. These shoes are great but, blimey, they're killing my feet.'

The two children walked down the alley, heading east of the Barrio del Carmen. When they reached the river and took the Puente del Real across it, they were greeted by the sweeping vista of the Jardines del Puente del Real, the lush and verdant gardens and nurseries unfurling like a luxurious, velvety green carpet.

'I hope no one's tried to make off with my cart,' Pepe remarked.

'Is it your father's?'

'Yes, but that's not what worries me. I'm more concerned about how Tomás, or Claw as you call him, would react to it. I don't know a lot about animals but he's wound up like a spring, that one.'

'That doesn't surprise me, after what he's learned,' Amparo replied. 'I feel bad about that. If only I hadn't written to him after the show . . .'

'He'd never have learned the truth,' interrupted Pepe. 'Would he really have been that much happier?'

'His parents left him in a convent, his adopted family left him to die in a fire . . .' Amparo reeled off.

'It might look that way on the surface, but we don't know for sure if that's what actually happened,' Pepe tried to reason. 'Anyway, if you'd never reached out to him, Tomás would have been forever asking himself, *Who are my real parents? Where am I from?* You've given him a way to find answers.

'I did it for myself,' Amparo admitted. 'To begin with

anyway.'

'But you're doing it for him now as well, aren't you?'

Amparo nodded.

Pepe jumped over a dung heap and screwed up his nose. 'Come, this way, we need to cross here.'

They left the Jardines del Puente del Real behind and walked down a quieter street.

'Going back to Tomás,' Pepe went on, 'he turned up at my house this morning with a right face on him. It looked like he'd come to give me a thrashing. In fact, my brothers were straight there, ready to jump in.'

'That's nice of them to protect you.'

'Nice, that bunch of delinquents?' retorted Pepe. 'Yeah, you're probably right. They can thrash me whenever they like but woe betide anyone else who tries. Anyway, Tomás wasn't there to hit me, he'd come to ask me to go out to the Trastamara estate with him tonight. So here we are. Oh, great, the cart's still there, I can see the mule too. As for the panther, well, that'll be around somewhere.'

Pepe had tethered the mule outside a well-lit *osteria*. When it saw Pepe, it brayed loudly.

'Shh, Stockfish, shhh,' Pepe scolded, untying the mule. 'Don't be drawing attention to us.'

'You called your mule Stockfish?' Amparo asked. 'Why would you do that?'

'Because it likes playing dead,' explained Pepe. 'You can't imagine how many times I've gone into the courtyard to get it, and there it's been, lying on the ground, stiff as a board, legs in the air like a stick insect.'

Amparo laughed at Pepe's absurd story. 'Only you could come up with something like that.'

The owner of the *osteria* – a man around fifty years old wearing a brown apron with the name of his restaurant – the *Barbacana* – embroidered on the front came out with his hands on his hips.

'Two men tried to make away with the animal,' he informed Pepe. 'But you should've seen how your mule bit into them to defend herself. She took one of their fingers right off.'

Pepe rubbed the mule's nose. 'Oh, you're a true Sorolla all right. Well done.'

The restaurant owner's face turned serious. 'I don't know where you're headed but watch out. There are a lot of rascals and rapscallions around.'

Pepe and Amparo climbed on to the cart. 'Of course, *señor*. Good evening,' replied Pepe, then turned and whispered to Amparo, 'Like there's anyone more rapscallion than us!'

The mule set off at a slow, steady pace. They left the city behind and ventured along a dusty, unpaved track, the buildings on either side fewer and further apart, and the light from them increasingly dwindling.

'I have a couple of lanterns,' Pepe mumbled, stopping the cart to fiddle around with something. A soft hiss followed by the flickering of a match revealed the interior of a rusty lantern. 'Here, you take this one. I've got another one for me.'

'Where's Claw?' asked Amparo, looking around. At that moment, something heavy jumped on to the back of the cart. Amparo let out an involuntary cry and only saw the panther when she turned around.

'He's right here,' Pepe commented, getting the cart moving again.

The country road was deserted and lacked any kind of sign or directions, but Pepe seemed sure they were going the right way. Sensing Amparo's confusion, he pointed ahead of them.

'That's Benimaclet up ahead. The Trastamara estate, or

what's left of it, is not far beyond that.'

They continued in silence, until Pepe finally cleared his voice.

'I've never asked you this, but when . . .'

Amparo looked at him.

'When was the first time you . . .'

'Not long ago. I was eight years old. Thankfully it was spring.'

'Why?'

'Because I hadn't left for school yet,' she explained patiently. 'It was half past six in the morning, and I'd just got up for breakfast. So I was at home, alone, with my grandfather. If it had happened in winter, when the sun rises a lot later, I would've been out in the street, and then . . .'

Amparo let the conclusion hang in the air and Pepe took a few seconds to formulate his next question.

'What did your grandfather do?'

'Nothing to begin with, he just looked at me. I was so scared. No, scared doesn't convey even the half of it. I skittered frantically this way and that around the house, banging into the rafters, the walls. I didn't recognise myself, it was as if my arms and legs were still there, only they weren't.'

Pepe nodded, lost in thought. 'There's a man down in El Cabanyal who lost his leg when it got caught in a plough. He's around eighty now. I stop to chat with him occasionally; he has so many interesting stories to tell. Well, the point is, he told me something similar once. That he wakes up during the night and can still feel his leg, even though it's not there.

'It's a horrible feeling.'

'Then what happened?'

'My grandfather finally managed to stop me, he held me tight and sang me a song, stroking my wings. It calmed me down, even if the next few hours were agony. I had no idea that I'd turn back into myself at sunset. Not even my grandfather could've imagined that.'

'What's it like to fly?'

Amparo smiled. 'It's . . . it's . . .' She shook her head. 'It's freedom. I can't think of any other way to describe it. It's also lonely. For me, anyway. Most birds fly in flocks, falcons don't.' She shrugged. 'That must just be my fate.'

'What?'

'To be alone. In one form or the other.'

'You said earlier you used to go to school.'

'Precisely. I *used to*. Past tense.'

'Did you have friends?'

Amparo thought about Emilia, Renata and Mirela: Mirela in particular, of the three, the one to whom Amparo had been closest. They had grown up together, from when Mariano had taken Amparo in to live with him.

'A few.'

'Did you not tell them about . . . ?'

Amparo shook her head.

'Why not?'

'They wouldn't have understood. They would have been scared.'

'Yeah, I guess they would,' Pepe agreed. 'But only to begin with. Maybe with time they would've understood. I did.'

'You're not like other people.'

Pepe perked up at the compliment, puffing his chest out. 'Thank you, I just do my best.' He grew serious again. 'But don't you miss them?'

'A little maybe, though all things considered, there are advantages to being alone,' Amparo replied. 'It's easier – you don't get hurt and you don't risk hurting anyone else.'

Pepe thought about this. 'Don't take this the wrong way, but that seems a bit like the coward's way out.'

'Coward's?'

'Yeah.'

'Maybe I'll change my mind when I get older,' mumbled Amparo, unsure.

They continued the journey in silence, arriving in Benimaclet, a small cluster of houses around a church, which had been decorated for a festival. They rode through, attracting curious stares from the village's inhabitants who were clearly not used to strangers. Claw had lain down in the back of the cart, blending into its dark wooden planks.

The road wound its way through a number of wide-open fields, but up ahead, looming against the cobalt-blue sky and illuminated by a particularly bright crescent moon, was a dark shapeless mass.

'Those are the gardens of the estate,' Pepe explained. 'There's a gate, but when my brothers came here years ago, the padlock and chain had been broken. I doubt they'll have been replaced.'

They pulled up outside the ancient residence of the Trastamara family. The estate and gardens were enclosed within a high brick wall, which was punctuated at regular intervals by majestic statues of winged lions standing guard. Pepe stopped the cart in front of the gate, climbed out and tethered Stockfish to one of the iron rings anchored in the wall. Amparo followed on his heel, then Claw leapt out silently.

Holding the lanterns up high in front of them, Pepe and Amparo swung the gates open and slipped inside, followed by the panther.

A paved pathway wound its way through what must've been a neat border once but was now just a tangled mass of thorns. Amparo noticed a round fountain off to the side of the path; ahead was a wrought-iron gazebo under which, she imagined, the Trastamara family must've spent many a summer afternoon sipping *horchata*.

    'There's the main house,' Pepe whispered a few seconds later.

The tower came unexpectedly into view from behind the canopy of a tall cypress tree. Amparo stopped, speechless: her nose filled with imaginary smoke and her ears with the remembered sounds of confused shouts and screams. She closed her eyes.

Pepe slowed down. 'Is everything okay?'

Amparo nodded. 'Yes. The tower has triggered some more memories. I was here, the night it caught fire. I'm sure of it.'

Pepe looked at Claw who was moving by their side like a shadow. 'This whole thing with you two never being human together is a right royal pain in the neck. If you could only speak to each other, half of our problems would be solved.'

The path came to an end in a large, semi-circular forecourt, the outside edge of which was lined with a series of decorative amphora planters. The Trastamara house looked out on to this space.

Even though the fire had destroyed most of it, the remains of the building still conveyed a sense of wealth and majesty. Embodying the characteristics of both a traditional rural estate and an urban mansion, the heart of the Trastamara residence was the square tower. Despite the dark and the ravages of the fire, the decorations around the windows and balconies were still visible.

Amparo and Pepe, followed by Claw, approached the large entrance cautiously. The double doors stood slightly ajar and Pepe, glancing over his shoulder to check the panther was still with them, nudged them open with his foot.

'Let's hope this place is not really haunted . . .' he muttered.

Inside was a square atrium, the central feature of which was a sweeping marble staircase that gracefully wrapped around the room. A magnificent crystal chandelier hung on a thick chain over their heads, catching the moonlight filtering through the tall windows.

Amparo looked around, shaking her head. 'This place is not saying anything to me.'

'We've only just arrived, give it time,' Pepe replied, walking over to a mirrored cabinet pushed up against a wall. He opened one of the drawers and shone his lantern over it to see inside. 'Well, look what we have here,' he said under his breath, slipping something into his trouser pocket.

'Pepe,' Amparo admonished. 'I don't think you should do that.'

'I'm just taking what I need,' he explained. 'I don't want to be rich, just enough to buy a decent pair of shoes – not that these aren't decent, of course – and so my father doesn't have to break his back fifteen hours a day in his shop. Do you know most of his customers don't even pay?'

In response to Amparo's questioning look, Pepe continued his rant. 'Yes, they tell him to put things on their account and he's got such a soft heart, that's what he does. Every now and then the odd rich city *señora* comes in and pays up front, but that doesn't happen every day.'

Amparo didn't feel she could protest any further so she turned around and pretended not to see what Pepe was doing.

Claw, on the other hand, had padded silently in beside her.

'Do you recognise this place?' Amparo whispered.

The panther moved his head, but Amparo wasn't sure how to interpret the gesture.

'How I wish we could speak to each other!' she cried in frustration.

'I just said the same thing!' Pepe commented.

Claw walked towards the stairs but Amparo remained where she was. Pepe joined the panther, his pockets packed full of loot.

'Are you not coming upstairs?' he asked.

She shook her head. 'No, I've never been here before, I'm sure of it. I want to go outside.'

'Well, I'm not letting you wander around this place on your own,' Pepe proclaimed chivalrously. 'There's still that wandering ghost to consider.'

The panther disappeared up the stairs while Amparo and Pepe

went back into the garden. Proceeding with great care and paying attention to where they were putting their feet, they began to explore.

'That must be the stables over there,' Pepe remarked, pointing to a low, rectangular building up ahead. 'They certainly treated themselves well, these Trastamaras.'

Amparo walked over to the stables, and for a fleeting second images flashed through her mind of them being gigantic, so much taller than her, colossal almost, along with images of the hooves of enormous horses and their powerful legs.

'I was little,' she said quietly. 'Everything seemed so big.'

The girl walked past the stables and explored deeper into the estate. Beyond a solitary stone arch, she caught sight of some small buildings that had escaped the flames. Modest constructions with only one storey and no more than two rooms in each.

As if in a dream, Amparo walked under the archway and made her way towards the last house on the right. Unlike the others, it had a small space at the front, enclosed by a low, uneven wall. A voice in her head began to speak to her at the same time as she felt a tingling in her right knee:

Oh, have you hurt yourself, my darling?

Don't cry, it'll be all right.

Come, let me dry your tears.

'I used to live here,' Amparo whispered.

'Really?' Pepe inquired.

'Yes.'

'Hasn't your grandfather ever told you?'

Amparo shook her head.

She walked around the house, paying close attention to the windows. There were three; two were broken, and on the third the shutters were securely fastened. Part of her wanted to go inside and see where she used to live – there was no doubt about that – whereas the other part was scared of what she might find. Or maybe *not* find.

'Look, there's another building over there,' said Pepe, lifting his lantern. 'It looks like a greenhouse.'

He set off towards it but stumbled on a tree root and fell on to his knees. As he hit the ground, a few of the items he'd pilfered from the mirrored cabinet fell out of his pockets and into the long grass.

'Oh, for crying out loud! These spoons are probably worth a fortune.'

Bent over, he began sweeping his hands through the grass, trying to recoup his treasure. Amparo looked away and turned her attention to the greenhouse instead. She had no memory of it; it couldn't have been somewhere she spent any time as a child.

'Pepe, I don't think . . .'

'GO AWAY!'

A shadow had emerged from the greenhouse, screaming at them and moving very quickly in Pepe's direction.

'The ghost!' he yelled, terrified. 'My brothers were right!'

'Watch out!' cried Amparo, but before Pepe could scramble to his feet, the shadow had struck him with the large stick it was carrying.

'GO AWAY!' it barked in a guttural voice. 'GET AWAY FROM HERE!'

Pepe took a couple more blows before he managed to react. Half running, half crawling, he tried to flee his attacker, but the shadow seemed to have no intention of letting him go.

Amparo initially froze then managed to grab hold of a stone, which she hurled at the shadow. She missed.

Pepe received another blow on the legs and he howled in pain. Amparo grabbed a second stone and rushed at the two figures. When she was close enough, she threw the stone at the attacker, hitting his head, which was hidden by a hood. The shadow spun around in fury, yelling, and swung the stick like a club, striking Amparo on the arm.

'Ouch!' she cried.

A deep roar suddenly shook the air. Taken by surprise and scared by the sudden, earth-shaking sound coming from the house, the shadow dropped the stick and backed away. Amparo rushed over to Pepe and, ignoring the pain in her arm, helped him to his feet.

'Claw!' she yelled, spotting the panther bounding through the overgrown vegetation. The shadow retreated further. When the panther finally leapt forth from the bushes, the shadow screamed in terror and ran off.

Claw reached Amparo and Pepe in two swift leaps. He was about to continue after the fugitive, but Amparo stopped him.

'Wait! What if he's got a rifle?'

'He would've used it already,' Pepe interjected, rubbing his shin. 'Oh, the pain . . .'

'I don't think he wanted to kill us, just scare us,' Amparo reflected. 'Although he might've acted differently, faced with a panther.'

'Well, let's not stay here then,' Pepe said. 'Let's go before he comes back. With or without a rifle.'

The two children, followed by the panther, hurried away from the Trastamara house. They climbed back on to the cart and Pepe clicked his tongue to get the mule moving.

'Giddy up, Stockfish, get us out of here.'

As they trundled along the road, Amparo glanced back at the boundary wall and large wrought-iron gate. She was certain, now. This place had once been her home.

CHAPTER 10

BOOM, BOOM, BOOM.

'Pepe, that friend of yours who visited yesterday is here.'

Don Sorolla's deep voice echoed around the whole house, reverberating as far as the shop downstairs. Its recipient, however, was the only one who apparently didn't hear.

'Pepe!'

Up in the attic, curled up on his mattress, cover pulled up around his ears, Pepe muttered something in response and rolled on to the floor.

'Coming, Father, coming,' he groaned.

Pepe dragged himself over to the door then painfully on to his feet. 'Wretched ghost, Holy Mother of God.' He summoned a couple of well-known saints and added a few more of his own before pulling on his top and making his way cautiously downstairs. The risk of falling and potentially adding even more pain to the excruciating levels he was already experiencing, terrified him. The king of El Cabanyal was not normally easily scared.

As always, Don Sorolla's shop was bustling and full of life. Four of Pepe's seven brothers were sitting around a table having breakfast, while Enrique and his father were busy behind the counter, lining up chorizos, jars of olives and bottles of wine.

'Aha! Nice of you to join us! Your friend is outside.'

'What an ugly mug you have today, Pepe,' Alonso joked.

'When is it ever not ugly?' Geroni fired back.

Pepe ignored them and headed for the door. Don Sorolla watched him go, worried. 'Wait a second, son.' He extracted an almond biscuit from a glass jar and handed it to him. 'Here, have this. You look like you need it.'

The unexpected gift attracted a barrage of objections from the other Sorolla brothers, Enrique included.

'Those biscuits are worth a fortune, they came all the way from Madrid.' Don Sorolla silenced them all with a wave of the hand. Enrique shrugged. 'Whatever.'

'Thank you, Father,' said Pepe before wolfing the biscuit down whole. He hobbled out of the shop and into a bright, beautiful morning. The sky was clear and a gentle breeze had carried in the scent of the sea salt from the coast. Pepe saw Tomás leaning against the wall on the other side of the street, arms folded, head down, deep in thought.

'Tomás,' Pepe called, crossing the road.

Dark eyes looked up from the dusty ground. 'How are you?'

'Alive,' Pepe replied, forcing a smile.

'I should've followed him.'

Pepe shrugged. 'I'm covered in bruises. They'll heal. I'm more worried about Amparo. She couldn't move her arm last night.'

'I should've followed him,' Tomás repeated, frustrated.

'To do what? Rip him to shreds? That wouldn't have helped either – we'd only have had to bury him as well. For the love of God, do you know how hard that would've been?'

Tomás's face took on a pensive expression. 'What if the man who attacked us was *that guy*, El Gris?'

Pepe shook his head. 'No, I don't think so. He just seemed a bit angry that we were poking around the estate. Maybe he's just some vagabond living there who doesn't want strangers under his feet.'

'Maybe,' Tomás conceded, although not very convincingly.

Pepe rubbed his side. 'Did you find anything when you went upstairs? In the Trastamara house, I mean.'

Tomás nodded. 'I managed to look around two rooms before I heard you guys screaming and rushed back downstairs. The first one seemed like a guest room because it was pretty bare. The second one, on the other hand . . .'

'The second one?' Pepe urged.

'It was mine.'

'No! Are you sure?'

Tomás nodded. 'Mine and my brothers',' he added. 'Although I can't really call them my brothers.'

'How did you . . . ?' asked Pepe, anxious to hear the rest of the story.

The other boy shook his head. 'The shape of the room, the position of the beds. The fire destroyed most of the contents but I recognised enough. My bed was the biggest and there was a sea landscape painted on the wall beside it.' Tomás gave a rare smile. 'It's funny, I've been unaware of that bed for ten years, but as soon as I saw it . . .' he snapped his fingers, 'just like that it all came flooding back.'

'We need to take another trip to the convent,' Pepe commented, thinking. 'After what Donna Manuela told us about El Gris, the Mother Superior clearly knows more that she's letting on. However, I do believe she's keeping schtum because she thinks it will protect you.'

'I don't need protecting. I'm not a child, I can look out for myself. It wouldn't be easy to kidnap me, neither as a child nor as a panther.'

Pepe agreed, looking Tomás up and down. 'You're right. But Amparo, on the other hand . . .'

'What does Amparo have to do with this?'

'She's just like you, isn't she? If this El Gris finds out, he might try to take her. She's not strong like you. Quite the opposite, she's much slighter and weaker in build. Trust me, my friend, I know what that's like!'

Tomás seemed to have suddenly realised the importance of what Pepe had just said. 'You're right. I need to stay away from her, don't I?'

'I don't think she'd take that well,' commented Pepe. 'You're trying to retrace your roots; she wants to know what happened prior to her grandfather taking her in when she was two years old. We know for certain that you both have shared elements of your past. She won't let you shut her out.'

'I don't want to turn my back on her, but I can't let her be seen with me if it will put her in danger.'

'On this we both agree. I'll be the go-between then.'

Tomás gave Pepe a questioning look. 'Why do you still want to help us? Didn't you get away with enough loot last night?'

Pepe scratched his shin with a foot. 'I'm hooked now. And as I said before, without me you two would be lost. I know everyone in this city. I am . . .'

'The king of El Cabanyal, I know, I know.' Tomás stood up from the wall. 'So what's the plan? Are we going back to the convent?'

'Yes. But won't someone at the fair start to wonder if you're missing? You missed the show last night.'

'I said I was ill,' Tomás replied.

'And they believed you?'

'I'm the Magic Lair's biggest money-spinner, they're not going to risk making me angry, are they?'

Pepe threw his hands up in the air. 'If you put it like that, let's go.'

They set off towards the city centre, along El Cabanyal's sunniest, liveliest streets. The journey took them through a busy market where they had to zigzag through stalls laden with fruit and vegetables, rolls of fabric, ceramic pots in all shapes and sizes, fishing tackle and lots more.

Every now and then they'd come across one of the *falla* sculptures – large, spectacular and surrounded by hordes of curious spectators and tourists – and they couldn't help but slow down to take a look for themselves.

'Hasn't anyone ever suspected anything? About your true nature, I mean?' Pepe asked when they moved away from the Calle Matias Perello sculpture.

Tomás shook his head. 'No. They all believe it's a true sleight of hand put together by me and my mum. Ester is the only one who knows the truth, but she'd never tell anyone. She's very loyal to Manuela.'

'Why?'

'Ester's parents worked in the Magic Lair but they died in a show in Madrid about twenty years ago. It was a terrible tragedy, more than fifteen people died. Ester had no other family so Manuela took her in. Then I arrived ten years later.'

'So Ester is like an elder sister to you?'

Tomás nodded. 'We don't really get on though.'

'Well, nothing new there!' exclaimed Pepe, laughing. 'It would be weird if you did. I consider myself an expert on the subject of older siblings.'

Tomás gave a half-smile.

'But,' Pepe resumed the conversation, 'isn't it risky letting all those people see you every night?'

'Not at all,' responded Tomás. 'It's the best way to prove I have nothing to hide.'

Pepe didn't seem at all convinced but let it go. The two boys had reached the road for Almassera. It was the day of *La Cremà*, when all the *fallas*, with the exception of the winning ones, would be set alight, and Valencia was busier than it had ever been, buzzing with tourists, countryfolk in town to see their city relatives, merchants looking to make some easy money.

Pepe and Tomás didn't have to wait long for a lift: a young peasant couple on their way home from delivering eggs and poultry to a number of restaurants in the city welcomed them up on to their cart. Naturally chatty and full of life, the couple made easy, non-stop conversation with Pepe, who seemed happy to have found such an enthusiastic audience for all his tales. Tomás, on the other hand, kept himself to himself in the back, arms folded and eyes gazing into space.

'Thanks for the ride and safe journey home!' a jovial Pepe called out when the couple left them just before the convent.

'Yes, thank you,' Tomás mumbled as he climbed out.

The two farmers gave Pepe a warm goodbye and pulled on the reins to get the mule moving again towards Albuixech, their home village.

'So far so easy,' Pepe remarked as he dusted off his socks. 'The hard part comes next.'

They walked up to the convent but instead of entering through the main gate like before, they walked around the building looking for another way in.

'There has to be one,' Pepe stated.

'How can you be so sure?' Tomás asked.

'Don't you remember how clean the entrance to the convent was?'

'No, to be honest, I didn't notice.'

'Well, I did and I can assure you that the floor hasn't

seen any muddy, dung-covered boots or baskets of fruit and vegetables and the like. And unless they're made of fresh air, even nuns have to eat.' Pepe advanced another few metres then pointed at something he'd spotted just ahead of them. 'See, what did I tell you. Right *again*.'

The king of El Cabanyal walked triumphantly up to a modest wooden door. On either side were stacks of wooden crates filled with fruit and vegetables. Two skinny cats circled them, waiting to swipe something a little more tasty.

'You wait here.' Pepe gestured to Tomás. 'I know how to get the sisters on side.'

'Wait.' Tomás stopped him. 'Tell me what you plan to do.'

'Have a root around in the Mother Superior's office.'

'You're mad.'

'I may well be, but there's little chance she'd receive us a second time, and even if she did, she wouldn't tell us anything new. So you sit tight out here and leave the hard work to me.

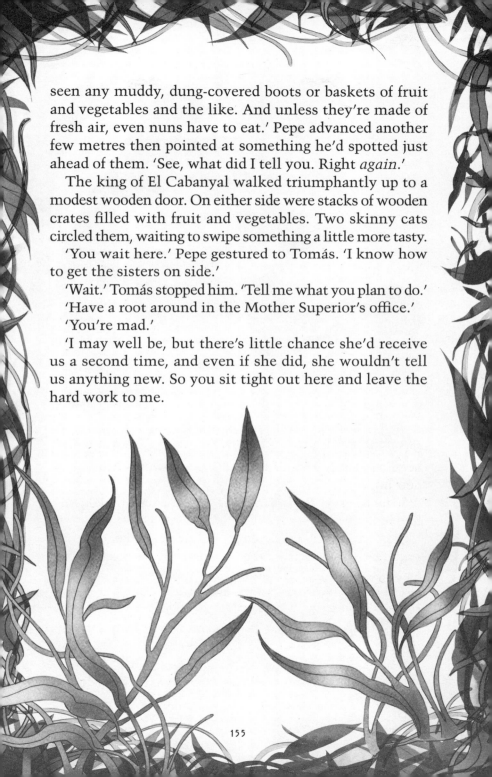

CHAPTER 11

CHAPTER 12

When Tomás saw Pepe re-emerge from the convent kitchens with two heavy tomes tucked under his arms, his jaw dropped in surprise.

'What on earth . . .'

'Run! Run!' Pepe ordered. With the agility of a rabbit, he hopped into the dense foliage then darted through the empty fields at top speed, yelling, 'Come on!'

Tomás gathered himself from the shock and set off after Pepe. The pair ran and ran, until Pepe was certain there were no furious nuns on their heels.

'You do know,' Tomás panted when they collapsed under a cypress tree to get their breath back, 'that it's a sin to steal?'

'Nothing has been stolen!' Pepe retorted adamantly. He nodded to the books. They have merely been borrowed. Anyway, with the Almighty,' he pointed to the sky with a thumb, 'I have an understanding. Everything will be explained when my time comes. Now let's see . . .' he picked up the books, 'if there's anything useful in here.'

'Where did you find them?'

'Locked in a drawer in the Mother Superior's desk. Luckily I also found the key. They weigh an absolute tonne.'

Pepe opened the first one. 'Um. This looks like an accounting ledger.'

Tomás leaned in to get a closer look at the pages. '*Refectory modernisation expenses, March 1897 . . .*' he read.

Pepe flicked quickly through to the end then pushed the book to one side. 'It's just one account after another. Let's have a look at the other one.'

He picked up the second book and opened it. The first two pages were blank but the third revealed an elaborate inked script, adorned with intricate curls and whorls, which said:

REGISTER OF ABANDONED CHILDREN

Pepe looked at Tomás, grinning triumphantly. 'See, what did I tell you?'

'It pains me to admit it, but I'm beginning to think you're a genius.'

Pepe cackled and went back to the book.

'Let's try and piece this together. It all seems pretty well laid out. *Date, sex, age, notes*,' he read. '18 March 1854, male, four weeks, mother deceased, father ill, no other living relative. Poor thing.'

'Go to 1900,' urged Tomás. 'That was probably the year I was left at the convent.'

Pepe flicked through the pages of the register. 'So many different handwritings,' he observed. 'Here we are, 1899, January 1900!'

The two boys scanned the pages carefully.

'Our Mother Superior was much more accurate than the ones before her,' Pepe noted. 'Have you seen how many comments and annotations she added?'

Tomás nodded without taking his eyes off the page.

'Let's hope she made a note somewhere of my birthmark. If she didn't, I don't know how I'll find myself among all these abandoned babies.'

'*February 1900; male, seven weeks, dark hair, blue eyes, mother and father living but destitute*,' Pepe looked at Tomás. 'What does destitute mean?'

'Very poor,' he answered simply. 'What does it say next?'

Pepe read the next line, '*Resident in Massamagrell*. I've heard of that, it's around here somewhere.'

'There's more,' Tomás noticed. 'In the margin.'

Pepe peered. 'What the blazes, it's barely legible.'

'Let me see.'

Brow furrowed in concentration; Tomás tried to decipher: '*Oct. 00 – ret*.' He thought about it for a second – *October 1900, returned* – and understood. 'It means that the parents left the child temporarily then returned to reclaim it in October of the same year.' He read further through the list, stopping every time he saw the word 'male'. As the number of scanned pages grew and grew, so did Tomás's frustration. 'For all I know, this could be me,' he snapped after a bit. '*Male, five weeks, dark eyes and hair, parents deceased, left by someone who knows the family*,' he read. 'Or this: *male, nine weeks, black hair, brown eyes*. It doesn't say who left the child though.'

Shaking his head, Tomás handed the book to Pepe and stood up. He began pacing back and forth.

'What a waste of time. I'll never find out who I am. What does it matter anyway? I ended up in that convent because my parents died or because they were too poor to take care of me. So desperately poor they couldn't even come back and get me. Tomás kicked a stone angrily, sending it flying into a tree trunk.

'Yes, yes, I see,' Pepe mumbled distractedly, continuing to scan the register. He worked in silence for a few minutes, becoming so engrossed he was unaware of Tomás's frustration and the repeated kicking of stones and tree trunks.

'We need to just give it back,' Tomás announced. 'The register, that is. It hasn't helped me but maybe someone else could . . .'

'If you'd just stop rambling, maybe I could focus a bit better,' Pepe said curtly. 'Found it!' He smacked a hand on the page excitedly. 'I've said it before – you need to have more faith. Look at this: *male, nine weeks, dark hair, birthmark under armpit.*'

'My birthmark's not under my armpit.'

'Because you've grown since then, haven't you! And the mark must've spread and shifted a little! Look what else it says.'

Tomás sat back down beside Pepe and took the book from him. '*Father deceased, mother living. Sagunto. Do not adopt.*' Tomás bit his lip. 'Do not adopt: that means my mother wanted to come back and get me!'

Pepe nodded vigorously. 'See?'

'Why didn't she, though? Why did I end up at the Trastamaras'?'

'Maybe . . . maybe in the meantime . . .'

'Yes, she might've died.' Tomás stared at the inked words on the page. 'Sagunto. That's where I'm from. That's where I want to go.'

Pepe nodded again. 'Good idea. Shall we go now?'

Tomás threw Pepe a perplexed look. 'Why do you want to come with me?'

'Do you have any idea how to get to Sagunto?'

'No, but I'll find someone who'll take me.'

'Ah, right. Because you definitely look like someone people would be over the moon to stop and pick up,' Pepe commented. 'You exude anger with the whole world, and yes, I know you have every reason to, but I doubt anyone would let you up into their cart with that miserable face of yours. I, on the other hand,' he said, flashing Tomás his most dazzling smile, 'am someone people cannot say no to.'

'You're mad. I've told you that already, haven't I?'

'Aren't we all a little mad?'

Tomás sighed. 'How far is it to Sagunto from here?'

Pepe stopped to think. 'Father and Enrique went to a famous bakery there once to pick up a basket of *ximos* . . .'

'*Ximos?*'

'Fried buns,' Pepe explained hastily. 'Do you know anything at all, Tomás? Anyway, back to my story. They went on the cart and it took them about an hour and a half. But we can't take my father's cart today as he sent Bartomeu and Nofrem to Picanya to pick up some cheese. I heard them talking about it yesterday. What we'll do is follow the Carraixet river to where it meets the coastal road. There's a constant stream of traffic up and down there, thanks to which . . .' he gave Tomás another broad smile, 'it will be easy as pie to get a lift.'

'Okay.' Tomás sighed, sounding exhausted.

The two boys stood up. Pepe had the register tucked under his arm and reached out to pick up the other book. 'I'll go and put these back.'

'How? Back through the kitchens? The nuns will roast you for lunch if they catch you.'

'Don't worry. Let's meet at the Almassera bridge in about twenty minutes. Do you remember how to get there?'

Tomás nodded and Pepe strode off confidently, disappearing back into the undergrowth.

CHAPTER 13

It was midday by the time Pepe and Tomás made it to Sagunto. The sun was high in the sky, and a gentle breeze from the sea invigorated the air.

'We're here,' announced the man who'd offered them a lift in his cart when he'd seen them making their way along the hot, dusty road on foot. He was carrying an unwieldy load of fine ceramics so, with no room in the back, the two boys had to squeeze in beside him up front. The awkwardness of the seating arrangements was offset, however, by the speed at which they travelled: the ceramic merchant's cart was no ordinary one, pulled by a simple mule – this one was drawn by a powerful horse, which trotted at a steady, deliberate pace for the entire journey.

Pepe jumped out of the cart. 'Thank you, *señor*. We wish you a good day.'

The man tipped his hat, pulled on the reins, and set off again along the road towards the port.

Standing at the base of a hill, Tomás looked up at the imposing castle perched at its summit, walls bleached white by the relentless sun.

'This way,' Pepe indicated. 'Let's find a tavern, maybe there'll be someone willing to chat.'

They headed for the centre of town, skirting the base of the hill.

Sagunto seemed unusually quiet and calm to Pepe and Tomás, after the buzz of Valencia.

'There's not a soul around,' Tomás noticed.

'Let's head for that bell tower,' Pepe suggested, pointing up ahead. 'Where's there's a church, there's usually a square. And where there's a square, there's usually a tavern or two.'

To get to the church in the town centre, they had to go down a narrow alleyway hemmed in on both sides by tall buildings, the walls a mix of pristine white and soft straw-yellow plaster.

'No one here either,' remarked Pepe. 'Maybe they've all hotfooted it to Valencia for the Las Fallas festival.'

It was only when they got to the end of the alley that they finally encountered another human: a grey-haired woman dressed in bright, colourful clothing. She was sitting with her back to the boys, outside what must've been her workshop, absorbed in painting on a large canvas that was mounted on a sturdy wooden easel.

When Pepe and Tomás walked past her, she looked up from her work and scrutinised them from head to toe.

'Good day,' Pepe greeted her courteously, stopping to admire the painting, which at that moment resembled a shapeless expanse of blue dotted with green.

'Good day,' the woman replied, her hands continuing to dance over the canvas.

'Could we ask you something, *señora* . . . ?'

'Señora Antonia,' she replied. 'What do you want to know?'

'We're not from around here,' Pepe began, and the woman's thin lips pressed into a gentle smile.

'I'd never have known.'

'Well, yes, it's true. We've come from Valencia looking

for information about a baby who disappeared in 1900 when he was only weeks old. His father was dead but we believe his mother was still living at the time.'

Antonia looked up from the canvas to study the two boys. 'A baby that disappeared almost fifteen years ago? I don't know how I could help you with that.'

'Are you sure?' Tomás asked.

The woman nodded.

Pepe flashed her a smile. 'Oh well, thank you all the same.'

The boys set off again and soon reached the church square. As Pepe had anticipated, there were a number of shops around it: a pharmacy, a food store, and a tavern with a few tables on the pavement outside it.

Tomás grabbed Pepe's arm. 'Over there, look,' he said, pointing to a grand house opposite the church. The facade was covered in fine white rendering, the walls decorated with rich stone carvings, delicate scrollwork framing the windows and a tapestry of wooden inlays adorning the grand wooden door. What had caught Tomás's eye though was not the architectural elegance but the line of statues gracing the roof.

'Winged lions! Just like the ones we saw at the Trastamara estate!' cried Pepe. 'They're so similar! No, not similar – identical, I'd say!'

'Hey, you two, come over here!'

Pepe and Tomás spun around. A group of four men playing cards and sipping *horchata* outside the tavern were watching them, cards in hand. The thinnest of the four, a man with rough, sun-darkened skin, a dishevelled beret on his head and a scraggly grey beard, had beckoned them over. He was playing with one hand, his other arm hanging by his side.

Pepe pointed to himself. 'Are you talking to us, *señor*?'

'Yes, I'm talking to you,' the man replied. 'Correct me if I'm wrong, but were you just talking about those lions up there?'

'You're not wrong,' Pepe replied affably. 'They're such beautiful sculptures, so meticulously detailed and . . .'

'. . . and cursed!' the man cried, banging his cards down on the table. 'Cursed, that's what they are. They cost me my arm, the wretched things!' He lifted his dangling arm with the other hand then let it go. It flopped, limp and inert. 'There, that's what those things cost me.'

Pepe and Tomás stood in silence, sensing that they were about to hear more.

'It was bucketing with rain that day,' the man began. 'Pouring down in torrents, it was, like nothing we'd ever experienced in these parts. But the boss wouldn't listen! The statues had to go up, no two ways about it, because he'd promised his client that their fancy new mansion would be ready to move into the very next day.'

The man's friends shook their heads and shared some mumbled words of outrage and support.

'I tried to reason with him, but no, he wasn't having it. I was to get up on to the roof or find myself another job. So up on to the roof I went.' The man let out a bitter, sorrowful laugh, filled with anger and regret. 'The next day the client moved into his lovely home with its beautiful winged lions as planned, whereas I . . .' he lifted his chin towards his limp arm, 'I had no arm and no job either. Because what use was a crippled labourer to the boss? That's what he called me, a cripple.'

'I'm so sorry, *señor*,' Pepe said. 'Truly sorry.'

'Oh, I'm not his only victim,' the man resumed. 'This place is full of people he wronged. Labourers who objected to the inhumane working conditions, craftsmen who were never paid on time . . . all of them met some nasty end or other. Every single one of them. The man was a criminal, of the worst kind.'

Pepe nodded pensively. '*Senor*, please excuse my directness, but is the person of whom you speak Don Ricardo Trastamara, by any chance?'

A flash of repressed rage flickered in the man's eyes. 'Yes, it was him. Damned scoundrel that he was. But he got what he deserved, didn't he? His house went up in flames, his wife left him and he lost everything. Everything.'

The men around the table mumbled their agreement and resumed the card game in silence.

'Trastamara,' Tomás whispered to Pepe. 'Can it possibly be a coincidence? That I come from here, that Trastamara had business in the town and then I was adopted by him.'

'I don't know,' Pepe reflected. 'Admittedly, it is strange.' He stepped towards the card table, but with a posture of humble submission and trying to conjure up an expression of remorse and genuine regret.

'*Señors*, forgive my insistence, but have any of you ever heard of a small boy who disappeared in 1900, when he was just weeks old? He may have been an only child, his father died before or right after he was born, whereas his mother was still living at the time.'

The four men shrugged their shoulders and offered mostly similar replies.

'No.'

'Never heard anything like that.'

'In 1900? Who remembers that far back?!'

Pepe and Tomás exchanged a quick glance, silently agreeing to try their luck elsewhere. They bid farewell to the four card players and set off for the pharmacy.

The man behind the counter barked rudely at them and threw them unceremoniously out of his shop, saying he had no time to waste with good-for-nothings like them.

'Have you ever seen such bad manners!' exclaimed Pepe, walking back along the road. 'Rude, self-important snail-eater of a man . . .'

They were treated a little better in the food shop but got nothing useful from its plump proprietor. She couldn't remember the child specifically. Back then the poor often entrusted their children to wealthy families or convents, she said.

Pepe and Tomás left the shop, demoralised.

'Let's try up at the castle,' suggested Pepe. 'Maybe we'll get lucky in that part of town.'

Visibly disappointed, Tomás nodded silently.

The two boys walked back along the road they'd come down. The painter was where they'd last seen her, sitting by her easel. This time though, she waved at them to stop when she saw them.

'You upset Ramiro, from what I've heard.'

Pepe threw his arms in the air. 'We certainly didn't mean to. How were we to know he was so bitter about Don Trastamara.'

'What do you two know about Ricardo Trastamara?' she asked, eyebrows raised.

'Not a lot,' Pepe replied. 'Just that he was rich and from what we've heard, treated his workers abysmally.'

'True,' the woman confirmed. 'Don Trastamara was infamous around here for his cruelty.' She let her gaze fall on Tomás, paying particular attention to the features on his face. 'Why did you ask about a child who disappeared from Sagunto in 1900?'

Tomás lifted his shirt to reveal the dark birthmark. 'Because I am that child, and I'm looking for my mother.'

Antonia stared in silence at Tomás's birthmark for several minutes. Then she closed her eyes and let out a deep sigh.

'You're just like her. Spitting image. Same hair, same

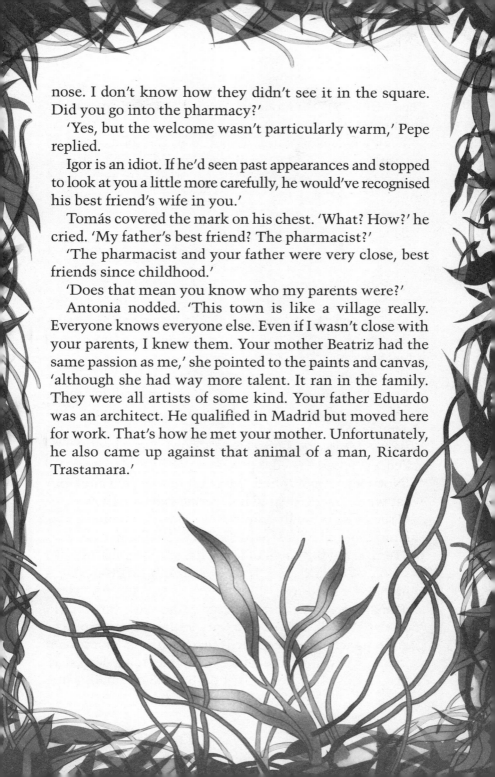

nose. I don't know how they didn't see it in the square. Did you go into the pharmacy?'

'Yes, but the welcome wasn't particularly warm,' Pepe replied.

Igor is an idiot. If he'd seen past appearances and stopped to look at you a little more carefully, he would've recognised his best friend's wife in you.'

Tomás covered the mark on his chest. 'What? How?' he cried. 'My father's best friend? The pharmacist?'

'The pharmacist and your father were very close, best friends since childhood.'

'Does that mean you know who my parents were?'

Antonia nodded. 'This town is like a village really. Everyone knows everyone else. Even if I wasn't close with your parents, I knew them. Your mother Beatriz had the same passion as me,' she pointed to the paints and canvas, 'although she had way more talent. It ran in the family. They were all artists of some kind. Your father Eduardo was an architect. He qualified in Madrid but moved here for work. That's how he met your mother. Unfortunately, he also came up against that animal of a man, Ricardo Trastamara.'

As she came to the end of her story, Tomás was silent, fists clenched.

'So that's how it went? Trastamara killed my father because he dared to challenge him?' he said.

Antonia nodded. 'Your father wasn't his only victim, although I realise that won't be much consolation.'

'Is that why my mother fled with me? For fear that Trastamara would make victims of us as well?'

Antonia nodded again. 'Everyone knew but no one dared speak of it. When you and your mother disappeared, we all feigned ignorance. Who knows, maybe it's just as well. If someone had found you, Igor for instance, it could have led Trastamara straight to you.'

'Wasn't Trastamara ever punished for what he did?' Tomás asked.

'Men like him are never punished.'

'Antonia, do you really have no idea where Tomás's mother might be?' Pepe interjected.

'No, how could I? I have no idea what she did after she left here. Just like I had no idea what had become of you,' she said, turning to Tomás. 'If you're here now looking for your mother, that tells me she didn't bring you up. Who raised you then?'

'The man who rendered me an orphan,' replied Tomás.

Antonia was clearly taken aback at this. 'I'm so sorry,' was all she managed to say. She stood up. 'Come with me. Let's go back to the pharmacy. If you want, we could ask Igor to tell you something about your parents. About your father? Would you like that?'

Tomás gritted his teeth and Pepe realised he was fighting back tears.

'Of course we'd love to!' he intervened jauntily, to divert the attention away from Tomás. He put his arm through the woman's and set off for the square. 'As we walk, Antonia,

maybe you could explain how you get your orange colour
so vibrant? I enjoy painting too, but I have to confess I
don't have an ounce of your talent.'

CHAPTER 14

It was almost time for the *La Cremà* part of the festival to commence. Valencia was preparing to set alight the hordes of wooden sculptures that had sprung up across the city, all except the winning ones. When Pepe and Tomás arrived at the Barrio del Carmen, the neighbourhood was already deep into the festivities: the Plaza del Angel sculpture, which Mariano had worked on, had come fifth in the competition.

'Seventy-five pesetas!' someone cried. 'It's a fortune!'

Calle Caballeros and the streets around it were teeming with life as people flocked to Plaza Pellicer to see the sculpture that had won the first prize of three hundred pesetas.

'We might as well give up,' Pepe suggested when they found themselves hemmed in by the crowds, unable to move. 'Amparo will be, you know, she'll be . . . well, we won't be able to have much of a conversation with her.'

'I want to see how she is,' replied Tomás, elbowing past people. 'And she can listen to what we have to tell her.'

Pepe was about to mumble something in reply when a surge from behind propelled him into the wall of a nearby building. Tomás cursed and reached out to grab Pepe by the shirt and yank him back.

'Surely there must be a shortcut?'

Pepe seemed to be thinking hard about this. 'No. We need to get to the turning for that alley. Amparo lives at the bottom of it, after the San Bartolomeo bell tower. This is the only way there.'

Tomás rolled his eyes and huffed in irritation but nevertheless held on tight to Pepe as the pair fought their way down to Calle de los Borja. Thankfully, it was less crowded than the main streets of the *barrio*.

They hurried along it, the air rich with the tantalising aroma of freshly fried churros, wafting from street traders' carts on every corner, and with the rich velvety scent of the melted chocolate the churros were dipped into.

'That smells so good, it's making me hungry,' Pepe muttered. 'If I don't eat something soon, I think I might die.'

'We'll have something later,' Tomás replied, marching ahead.

'Oh yes, I'll believe that when I see it. Next up you'll be telling me you've booked a seaside restaurant for a plate of paella,' Pepe retorted sullenly.

They walked for another few minutes until Amparo's house finally came into view.

'Something's going on,' Pepe noticed straight away. 'All those people seem worried.'

'Is that Amparo's grandfather?' Tomás asked, pointing to Mariano.

'I think so.'

Mariano was standing in the doorway of his house, talking agitatedly to Don Sebastià. People were clustering around them. Pepe and Tomás ran towards them and began to pick up fragments of Mariano's comments the closer they got.

'. . . door forced open . . . broken vase . . . chairs knocked over . . . feathers on the floor . . .'

'I don't know what to say, Don Mariano, there's so much commotion around,' replied Don Sebastià.

'I was gone for ten minutes, no more!' cried Mariano, sounding distraught. 'Who could've taken my falcon? And why would they take it?'

'Did your granddaughter hear anything?'

'Amparo's in bed unwell,' Mariano responded curtly. 'She wouldn't have heard a thing.'

'Forgive me, *senõr*s.' Pepe pushed his way through the throng of concerned neighbours. 'Pardon me. Thank you. Very kind. Appreciate it. So sorry.'

'You're Amparo's friend, aren't you?' Don Sebastià recognised Pepe.

'What friend?' Mariano asked, suspicious, turning to look at Pepe.

'I met your granddaughter at the fair,' Pepe improvised. 'I came by to say hello, that's all, but if now's not a good time I can . . .'

'It most definitely isn't,' Mariano snapped. He turned on his heel and went back into the house, slamming the door behind him.

Don Sebastià shook his head, distressed. 'Poor man. He loves that falcon almost as much as his granddaughter. But I really didn't see anything . . .'

'When did it happen?' Tomás interjected.

'Not too long ago,' the man replied. 'Don Mariano came back from his workshop with the falcon, he left it in the house and went back out again for a few minutes. I was at home with Tiano, I was getting ready to go to Plaza del Ayuntamiento . . .'

'Did the dog bark at all?' Tomás insisted.

'No, he was eating. He hears nothing and sees nothing when he has food under his nose.'

Tomás and Pepe looked at each other, concerned.

'Surely someone must've noticed something out of the ordinary? Like a stranger hanging around outside the house?' Pepe tried again.

'It's the day of *La Cremà*, son!' said a well-dressed man, wearing a hat and carrying a cane. 'Valencia is full of strangers!'

'Don Perell is right,' Don Sebastià said quietly. 'We can't ask the beggar either, the one that's always here beside my front door. He seems to have disappeared.'

Tomás and Pepe both turned to look where Don Sebastià was pointing, as if it might give them a clue as to what had happened.

'What's going on here? What are you all doing outside

Don Mariano's house? Is he sick?' A woman with thick dark hair, plaited and pinned on top of her head, and large gold hoops adorning her ears, pushed her way through the throng of neighbours and onlookers using her shopping bag as a battering ram. Once she had secured a spot alongside Don Sebastià, she pressed him again for an answer.

'So what's happened?'

'Don Mariano's falcon has disappeared, Donna Consuelo,' he replied. 'Someone broke into their house, there are signs of a struggle. Did you notice anything strange outside the house today?'

'You can't turn for strange folks in Valencia today,' Donna Consuelo retorted.

'I said the same thing,' stated Don Perell calmly.

'But . . .' the woman continued.

'But what?' Pepe asked.

The woman threw him a suspicious look. 'And who might you be?'

'A friend of Amparo's,' replied Don Sebastià quickly.

'And you too?' she insisted, pointing at Tomás.

'I'm a friend of Amparo's too,' he replied, struggling to contain his nerves and mask his impatience under her scrutiny. 'Can you tell us if you saw anything strange?'

Donna Consuelo folded her arms over her chest. 'What reason might you have to be so interested in Don Mariano's falcon?'

Tomás was on the verge of replying but Pepe was faster. 'We know how much Don Mariano and Amparo love their falcon. We'd be happy to help you find it.'

'Hmm.' Donna Consuelo raised her eyebrows and gave the boys a discerning gaze. Satisfied, she decided to give them the answer they were looking for. 'When I came past here on my way to the central market, I saw a man. A tall, thin man in dark clothing and with longish hair. I saw him from behind initially. He was giving some coins to the beggar, the one usually stationed outside your door, Don Sebastià.'

'Did you see his face at all?' Pepe asked. 'The tall man, I mean.'

'Oh yes. And let me tell you, he had a face that looked like it'd been etched by the hand of darkness, the devil himself. Not ugly, just . . . pure evil. The face of evil. Thank God it was only for a few seconds. The minute our eyes crossed, I turned and fled. God only knows how the beggar wasn't scared when the man bent down to speak to him.'

Pepe and Tomás looked at each other, aghast at what they'd just heard.

'We need to go.' Tomás grabbed Pepe's arm and dragged him away from the group of onlookers outside Amparo's house.

'G-g-goodbye . . .' Pepe managed to stammer to Don Sebastià and Donna Consuelo. 'If we find the falcon . . .'

'Stop wasting time!' Tomás scolded him. 'It was him. El Gris,' he said, elbowing his way through the crowds of people filling the streets.

'I know,' Pepe replied. 'The Mother Superior was right. He really is back.'

'Why did he take her and not me?'

Pepe shook his head. 'Who knows. I wonder how he managed to find her. What should we do? We don't know where he's taken her, or if he . . .'

'Let's go and talk to my mother. Maybe she'll have an idea, some advice, anything to help us understand where he might've gone.'

'She hasn't seen him in over forty years . . .' Pepe argued.

'Do you have a better idea?' Tomás bit back.

'No,' Pepe had to admit.

It took the two boys nearly an hour to get to El Cabanyal. Valencia was abuzz with activity. The main streets brimmed with a relentless tide of pedestrians; carts and carriages strained to push their way through the throng; horses neighed nervously and frustrated coachmen hurled expletives and curses at anyone in their way. In every neighbourhood of the city, vibrant sculptures had sprung up like beacons, their surfaces gleaming under the low rays of the setting sun, which was dipping behind the grand silhouette of the nearby buildings. Crowds of spectators and onlookers had gathered around each of the masterpieces.

Once through the brightly lit archway and into the fair itself, Tomás and Pepe hurried as fast as they could to the area where the wagons were located, behind the Magic Lair.

'Something's up,' Tomás cried, the minute he set eyes on the group of people huddled around Donna Manuela's wagon. He raced over to it, shouldering people out of the way, bounded up the steps and threw the door open. Pepe followed hot on his heels with his heart in his mouth.

Donna Manuela was in bed, face pale and body trembling. Ester was sitting beside her, patting the older lady's forehead with a damp cloth.

'What's wrong?' asked Tomás.

Ester threw him a look of reproach. 'You know it's not good for her to worry. The more she worries, the worse it gets. Where have you been? She's been asking for you all day.'

'I . . . I . . .'

'You, you, you, that's all it ever is. Always about you,' Ester snapped.

'Tomás,' Donna Manuela whispered, opening her eyes. 'Is that you?'

Ester stood up. 'I'm going to fetch some fresh water. Don't upset her, I'm warning you,' she ordered imperiously before leaving the wagon.

'Mother, I'm here. It's me.' Tomás kneeled by the bed and took one of his mother's clammy hands in his.

Donna Manuela turned her head painfully to look at him. Her hazelnut eyes were etched with a mix of emotions, from pain and concern to lingering regret. Pepe hung back beside the door, head tipped.

'You're all grown-up, now. A man, almost,' she murmured softly, lifting a trembling hand to try to caress his cheek. But her arm halted midway, before it dropped back on to the mattress with a soft thud. 'And I'm so old and weak,' she gasped.

'You're not old, Mother,' Tomás replied. 'You'll get better soon, you'll see.'

'No. There's no cure for what I have, we both know that.' Donna Manuela turned her head towards the portrait of the hazily outlined man on the wall by her bed. 'He was here.'

'Who?' asked Tomás.

'Julio,' she replied. 'El Gris.'

Tomás and Pepe looked stonily at each other.

'When?' Tomás questioned.

'Just now. He said he has something that's important to you and that you can get it back at the house with the tower.'

'Are you sure? Did he really say that?'

'Who said what?' Ester barked as she bustled back into the wagon with a pail of water.

'The man who was here before,' Tomás began, but Ester rudely interrupted him again.

'There was no man here,' she proclaimed.

'But she said . . .'

'She's been feverish and babbling all day,' Ester said curtly. 'Ever since you disappeared this morning. I'd like you both to leave now. I need to change her and give her her pills.'

Tomás kissed his mother's hand. 'I'll see you later.'

Donna Manuela mumbled something incoherent then closed her eyes, her breathing short and raspy.

'Out,' hissed Ester. 'Now.'

The two boys left the wagon.

'Did you hear that?' Tomás asked Pepe.

Pepe nodded. 'Amparo's at the Trastamara estate. What do you want to do? Should we let her grandfather know? Should I ask my brothers to . . .'

Tomás shook his head. 'No. I need to go there alone.'

'Alone?'

'It's a trap El Gris has set. He has no intention of freeing Amparo. Don't you remember what my mother said? El Gris kidnaps children who transform. He's using Amparo as bait. Because he wants me too.'

'Genius,' Pepe commented sarcastically. 'And from this you have deduced that the most sensible course of action is to go to the trap alone? What do you plan to do when you get there?'

'I don't know.'

'Well, I'm coming with you.'

'No, you're not.'

'Yes, I am.'

'I said no.'

'And I said yes.'

Tomás was about to insist further but Pepe jumped in first. 'I'll stay out of sight, I promise. El Gris won't even know I'm there. If he captures you as well, I'll be able to follow, see where he takes you, then go and get help. You're not in this alone, you know – we have to think about Amparo. She's my friend and I don't abandon my friends.' Not convinced, Tomás stood in silence. Pepe took advantage of this to have a look around. 'Listen, you folks don't happen to have horses around here, do you? Because a horse would come in very handy right now, if we want to get out to the Trastamara estate sharpish.'

Tomás nodded. 'Come with me.'

CHAPTER 15

The gate to the Trastamara estate lay wide open.

Pepe had clung on to Tomás as tight as he could for the entire ride, terrified he'd fall off and break a leg or, worse still, break his neck. On arriving at their destination, he pointed a trembling finger at the entrance: a dark carriage and four ebony-coloured horses stood there.

'It looks like the carriage of the devil himself. That's not a good sign.'

'Oh, it is, it is,' Tomás replied. 'The sooner we get to the bottom of this story, the better. Now let me go, will you? We can't get down off this horse with you wrapped around me like this.'

'No?'

'No.'

Reluctantly, Pepe detached himself from Tomás. However, without the other boy to hold on to, he then flung himself flat along the animal's back.

'I'm still holding the horse by the reins, dafty.' Tomás sighed. 'It won't throw you. Just get down, will you?'

Pepe released himself, sliding unsteadily down the horse's flank. The second he felt his feet touch the ground though, he heaved an enormous sigh of relief.

Tomás went off to tie the horse to the gate, beside the carriage. The sun was beginning to dip on the horizon and a cold, wet mist – unusual for the time of year – had descended on the estate, cloaking it in a veil of sadness.

Tomás set off along a path through the undergrowth, Pepe following at a safe distance, diving behind tree trunks to remain hidden.

Moving silently and unsure what they might find, they finally reached the main Trastamara house. Tomás looked around but nothing moved and only silence could be heard. He circled the building then headed out to the cottages that once housed the Trastamara servants. On seeing the small brick buildings, especially the one at the end with a low stone wall enclosing a tiny garden, he felt a rush of nostalgia, then refusal, but ultimately fear. Part of him wanted to go inside, but he forced himself to walk past. He continued on to the large greenhouse up ahead. As he reached the entrance to the glass and steel structure, he glimpsed a shadow moving inside.

'I'm here,' he announced.

The door to the greenhouse opened and a corpulent figure stepped into the gardens, dressed in a long, tattered cape darkened by layers of grime and dirt. Pepe, from his hiding place a few metres away, concealed within a tangle of plants and bushes, scrutinised him carefully.

Judging from the man's build, he couldn't have been that tall. He took a few steps towards Tomás.

'At last,' he rasped.

'You're not El Gris,' Tomás observed warily. 'I'm here to see him.'

'Oh, he'll be here soon,' the man replied, 'with that wretched bird.' He raised his arm and lifted the sleeve of his tunic, revealing the back of his hand. Thick, dark hair covered the skin, but cutting through it was a long scarlet line – a gash stretching from one side of the hand to the other. 'Getting hold of that thing was a nightmare. To think I used to believe it was a docile creature. I even stroked it once. Years ago, when the carpenter gave me a pair of his old socks.'

Pepe narrowed his eyes, then had to bite back an exclamation of surprise.

The beggar! he thought. *That's the beggar I saw outside Amparo's house!*

'Why are you helping El Gris?' Tomás asked. Unlike Pepe, he was unaware of the man's true identity, believing him to be no more than a stranger.

The man pushed his hood back to reveal a face obscured by a thick, dark beard and a mane of wild, untamed hair.

'You don't remember me, do you? Yet there was a time when you once called me Father.'

Tomás remained in silence while Pepe, crouched in the bushes behind, blurted out an astonished curse followed by a humble apology to the Almighty.

'So you are Ricardo Trastamara. The man who took me away from the Sant'Ignazio convent,' Tomás said.

'I didn't pick you, my wife Elsa did,' he clarified. 'I would never have had a child not of my own blood living with us. But she was so sad, so unconsolable, I had no choice. I had to do it to make her happy.'

'Didn't you ask the Mother Superior where I came from?'

Trastamara shrugged. 'No. Why would I? You were the son of some down-and-out somewhere.'

'That's where you're wrong.'

Trastamara tilted his head to one side, eyes narrowing as he scrutinised Tomás. 'What do you mean?'

'You used to build mansion houses in Sagunto years ago, didn't you? Well, there was a man there, in Sagunto, far more intelligent and capable than you. A young architect from Madrid. His name was Eduardo Ávila.

'Eduardo Ávila . . .' Trastamara echoed, deep in thought. 'Yes, I remember him well. He had the gall to challenge my methods. Several of my men rebelled because of him. He could've ruined me, if I'd let him.' Trastamara stared at Tomás. 'What do you know about him?'

'He was my real father.'

Trastamara was left momentarily speechless. Until he erupted in uproarious, uncontrollable laughter; a coarse, guttural sound that seemed almost animalistic.

'You, you . . .' he stammered, drying his eyes. 'You're that man's son? And I, of all people, am the one who saved you from that lurid orphanage, lavishing years of wealth and luxury upon you?' Trastamara burst into more laughter, flabbergasted at the irony of the situation. 'Oh my word, killing you is going to be so much more satisfying now.'

'I should be the one to kill you,' Tomás replied calmly. 'To avenge my father.'

Trastamara pointed a finger at him. 'No. I'm the one who deserves retribution for everything you took from me: my wife, my children, my beautiful home. All because . . . you are a monster.'

'I'm not the monster.'

'No?' Trastamara gave an evil smile. 'Who, then, gouged his baby brother's eye out? Who almost ripped the hand off their two-year-old sister?'

Tomás said nothing.

'Oh, nothing to say now, have we? What could you possibly have to say though?'

'I don't remember ever harming anyone . . .' Tomás replied, his voice cracking with uncertainty.

'Well, I do!' Trastamara screamed. 'I remember it like it was yesterday. You . . . you transformed . . . in front of us . . . into a beast, an untameable, uncontrollable beast.'

'I was scared. I didn't know what was happening to me . . .' Tomás spluttered.

'You attacked us all. Me, my wife, my children. *My beloved children*. So I turned my rifle on you one day, but you fled. I followed you to the hellhole those two degenerates lived in.' He pointed to the house with the walled garden around it. 'Right there. You were friends with the daughter, you spent a lot of time together. You sought refuge there and those two idiots got involved! They knew nothing of what had happened – I was just the big, bad villain in their eyes – and they chose to defend an animal over obeying me.' Trastamara laughed. 'So I got rid of them. But you managed to escape and then the fire broke out . . .'

Still hiding in the bushes, Pepe was struggling to believe what he'd just heard, his thoughts spinning and whirling around like a high-speed carousel. *Amparo was right: she used to live here, on the estate, with her parents, in the house that Claw sought refuge in that night. And Trastamara killed not just Tomás's father but Amparo's parents too.*

'When I got back to the house, the whole place had gone up in flames. Those traitors that worked for me had picked that very night to destroy me,' Trastamara continued. 'Elsa and the children had gone. The day after, someone told me they'd seen her in a carriage travelling through the city. Apparently, she'd jumped at the chance to get away from me.' He cleared his throat. 'No one would help me, despite all the work I'd given others over the years. To hundreds of men. Yet they all turned their backs on me and I ended up on the street.'

'I'm not surprised,' Tomás stated. 'You're a cruel, horrible man. You deserve what happened to you. And if I was part of it then I'm proud of that.'

Trastamara did not reply. Moving with deliberate slowness, he reached beneath the folds of his cape and pulled out the long rifle hidden beneath.

'Careful what you say, boy. The other night, when I surprised you poking around here, I wasn't armed. But as you can see, I am now.'

'So it was you, then. The person who attacked us.'

'I should've killed you. All three of you.'

The sound of steps approaching cut through their conversation. Pepe edged a little further forward then found a new spot to hide behind a tree trunk. El Gris walked out from around the side of the greenhouse. He was tall and thin, with a sharp, angular face, long, unkempt hair, and a predatory look in his deep-set, feral eyes. He gave the impression of a man driven by a single, grim purpose: to cause pain.

The falcon, with a stone tied to one leg, was locked in a tiny cage that El Gris carried in one hand.

Tomás clenched his fists when he saw the caged bird. Pepe prayed he'd be able to control himself.

He needs to stay calm, Pepe thought. *Or he'll never get out of this alive.*

'We finally meet.' El Gris addressed Tomás.

He stepped closer, then stopped, keeping his distance from Trastamara. Pepe caught the look of disgust the new arrival threw the former estate owner and couldn't help but wonder how the two of them had ended up in this treacherous alliance.

'Yours was the last one, you know,' El Gris continued.

'The last what?' Tomás barked.

El Gris set the cage on the ground and delved a hand into his coat pocket. He pulled out a large object, the size of an apple, and showed it to Tomás.

'What's that meant to be?' Tomás asked defiantly.

'The key to my freedom,' El Gris replied. Pepe leaned forward to hear more, risking being spotted, but El Gris and Trastamara both had their gaze trained on Tomás and didn't notice.

A wooden figurine, Pepe discerned. *But what's it supposed to be, I wonder.*

'An artist,' El Gris explained. 'It's the statue of an artist. Whereas this . . .' he pulled another figurine from his coat pocket, the same colour and size as the first one, 'is a carpenter.'

'I don't understand,' Tomás said. 'Maybe I don't want to either.'

'Oh, I think you'll find my story very interesting.'

'I know your story. My mother Manuela told me.'

For a fleeting moment, El Gris' face was a canvas of shifting emotions that Pepe struggled to decipher. Was it regret, pain or perhaps anger he saw? The harsh contours of El Gris' face made it difficult to pinpoint exactly what he was feeling. If he was even capable of feeling.

'Manuela didn't know the full story,' El Gris replied, back to his cold, composed self. 'For instance, she never knew that when I went to that village, forsaken by both man and God himself, I took the gold key from a statue. The statue of a man with a long stick. The statue of a wayfarer.'

El Gris turned the figurine over in his hands and fell silent for a moment.

'What I didn't realise was,' he continued, 'that it was a man, not a statue.' Pepe sensed a slight tremble in El Gris' voice as he shared this last revelation, 'and that when I took the key from him, he said I could keep it, provided I brought him the smile of the woman waiting for me outside the village.'

'Manuela,' Tomás murmured.

'He was just a poor wayfarer, old and weak. I assumed he was mad, so I said yes. But I lied.'

El Gris gave an empty smile.

'At dawn the next day,' El Gris resumed, 'when I woke up beside the gold that was to be my ticket to success, my way out of the misery I was born and brought up in, I realised it straight away, I *felt* different, I had changed. I ran back to the village with my cape over my head. The wayfarer was in the same place, the same position that I'd come across him the previous day.' He shook his head slightly. 'I didn't have to ask. The minute he saw me, he said I'd been as silly as those before me, the former inhabitants of the now deserted village. That's when he told me his story.'

Pepe glanced up at the sky: the sun was preparing to set. He wondered what Trastamara would do, faced with the panther, in only a few minutes time.

'He told me that the village,' El Gris recounted, 'had once thrived as a beacon of artistry and craftsmanship. Its talented, industrious inhabitants drew admirers from distant lands, eager to acquire their creations. Wealth flowed into the village, leading to a proliferation of grander homes and increasingly elegant squares. The wayfarer arrived in the village one day. He walked down the elegant main street, admired its paved stones, wandered through the ornate main square. However, when the villagers caught sight of him, they told him he must go. The marquis of Valencia would be gracing their village and the townsfolk wanted every detail to be perfect. The wayfarer left, but only after he'd issued the warning: *Fools judge with their eyes, the wise with their hearts*.'

Tomás shifted uneasily from foot to foot. 'I don't understand what any of this has to do with me or the falcon.'

'You're about to find out,' responded El Gris. 'The village was hit by a violent storm that night. By the time it ended, all the first-born children of the families who'd thrown the wayfarer out had turned into animals. A curse had befallen the village.'

The falcon beat its wings and let out a high-pitched squawk which El Gris ignored.

'The children would transform either by day or by night, without warning,' he continued. 'The village gradually withdrew from the world, its isolation growing as unsettling rumours about its inhabitants began to spread. Fearful that their children might be accused of witchcraft or worse, the families made the painful decision to leave. They dispersed to different corners of the country, each family keeping their destinations hidden from one another.

'So I'm from one of those families?' Tomás concluded.

'Yes. Upon concluding his tale, the wayfarer handed me a series of intricately carved wooden statues, each one a representation of the families from the village. He made it clear that if I succeeded in locating their descendants, he would restore me to my original form. And this . . .' El Gris raised the figurine of an artist, 'brought me to you.' He turned to the falcon and raised the statue of the carpenter. 'And this one to you. Your ancestors were talented carpenters. The best in the whole of Alicante.'

The falcon beat its wings again, agitated.

'Oh, the sun is setting,' El Gris noticed. He bent down to open the cage and yanked the falcon out by its legs.

'Be careful,' Tomás exclaimed. 'You'll break them!'

El Gris ignored him and placed the falcon – complete with the stone it was tied to – on the ground. Then he turned to Trastamara. 'The girl's clothes?'

The man extracted a bundle from under his filthy cloak and tossed it carelessly at the falcon.

'Dear Tomás, it's been a pleasure talking to you,' El Gris concluded. 'But my freedom awaits.'

'What about Manuela?' Tomás countered. 'I'm like a son

to her. Do you really want to cause her any more pain?'

His expression turned to ice. 'Manuela made it very clear what she thought of me. She said she loved me, saw me for my true self. That morning, many years ago, her actions told a very different tale.'

'She didn't . . .' Tomás began, but at that very moment, the sun dipped behind the trees.

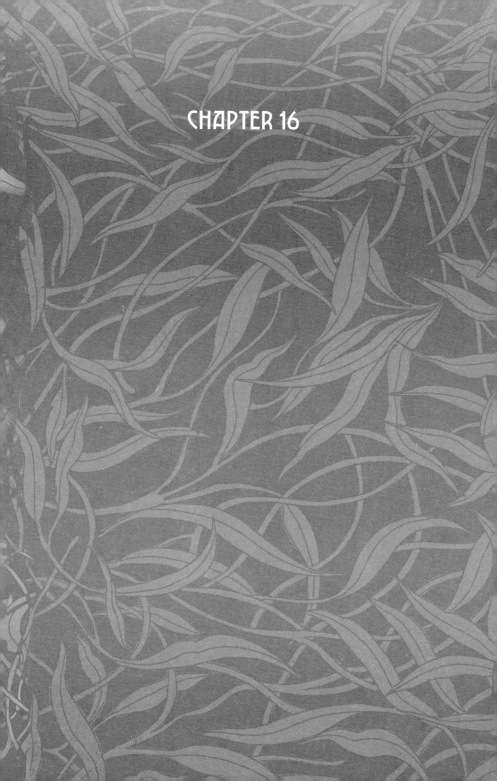

CHAPTER 16

Trastamara aimed his rifle at the panther.

'Not yet,' El Gris ordered. 'His life belongs to the wayfarer.'

'But you told me, you promised!' Trastamara protested.

'I promised you no such thing,' El Gris proclaimed, his voice so icily resolute it was clear the matter was not up for debate. Trastamara kept his rifle trained on the panther.

Amparo, still dazed from the transformation, hurried to cover herself then raced over to Claw. She placed herself firmly between the panther and Trastamara.

'Get out of the way, you stupid girl,' Trastamara ordered.

'Why? What will you do? Shoot me like you shot my parents?'

Trastamara looked at Amparo, confused. 'I have no idea what you're talking about.'

She pointed to the small cottage she was born and brought up in. 'I'm talking about the man and woman who lived there. My mother and father.'

'Ha ha, so history repeats itself,' he cackled. 'You want to die for that animal too?'

'Taking the panther's life won't get you anything; it can't return what you lost through being so ruthless and foolish.'

'Foolish?' Trastamara echoed, outraged. 'How dare you? I'll shoot you both!'

'I told you already, their lives *do not belong to you*,' El Gris enunciated each word slowly and deliberately, in the iciest of tones. 'Lower your weapon.'

'I don't take orders from anyone!' Trastamara yelled angrily. 'Least of all from a fairground freak like you!'

El Gris spun around to face Trastamara. With the speed and precision of a striking snake, he leapt at the man and seized the rifle with one hand. Simultaneously, his other hand shot out and clamped on to Trastamara's arm, twisting it sharply with a single, abrupt movement.

'Aaaarghh!'

Trastamara shrieked. 'You've broken my arm, you've . . . !'

El Gris grabbed Trastamara by the frayed collar of his tattered cloak. 'Not. Another. Word. Or it will be your last.'

Curled up on the ground, Trastamara whimpered a series of indistinct mutterings while cradling his arm. El Gris took aim at Amparo and the panther.

'Come with me. The wayfarer awaits you.'

'Where?' Amparo asked.

'Where it all began.'

With the rifle pointed ominously at them, Amparo and Claw began the walk towards the gate. The sky above them darkened and the air grew thick with the sounds of the evening. The mournful hoot of a distant owl pierced the quiet, and for the first time ever, Amparo wished not to be in human form.

'Stop,' El Gris ordered when they reached the carriage. His eyes never leaving them, he opened the small wooden door, reached in with one hand and grabbed something metallic that jangled eerily in the dark. Rifle still trained, El Gris closed the distance between them and handed Amparo a pair of horseshoe-shaped handcuffs joined by a heavy chain.

'Put them around your ankles.'

Amparo obeyed, reluctantly.

El Gris handed her another pair of handcuffs with a much longer chain. 'Restrain the panther's legs.'

The girl took the handcuffs, her mind racing. She wondered if there would be a sliver of opportunity to escape once they were inside the carriage. Maybe, just maybe, they could leap out into the street or shout for help if they happened to see someone nearby. Desperation fuelled her thoughts. She clung to them, needing to believe that there was still hope for her and Claw, that it wasn't all over.

'I'm so sorry,' she whispered as she secured the cuffs around the panther's legs.

'Get in, quick.'

Peering inside the carriage, Amparo realised it was an inky-black void. Swallowing the lump of fear in her throat, she inched hesitantly towards the step, but before she made it, the silence was broken by the sound of hooves.

'Get in, now!' El Gris shouted again.

Amparo defied the command and remained rooted to the spot. She stood instead on tiptoe, neck stretched forward, eyes squinting against the encroaching gloom, filled with a sudden hope.

'I said . . .'

The outline of a horse became discernible in the distance. It was advancing at speed and, to Amparo's great joy, it was heading for the estate!

'Help!' she shouted. 'Help!'

'Quiet!' hissed El Gris. 'Be quiet!'

But the animal had come to a stop by the carriage already. A striking beige specimen with sandy hues, the horse had a distinctive white star in the centre of its forehead. Its back and flanks were adorned with light markings, and on its back sat two women. Amparo recognised them both.

Donna Manuela, wrapped in a heavy cloak, face ashen and twisted in pain, murmured something to Ester, who was holding the reins. The younger woman dismounted then held out an arm to help the other woman down. She displayed no sign of fear towards the rifle or the panther, nor did the presence of El Gris seem to unsettle her.

Donna Manuela looked up. She took in the panther first, then Amparo, then finally let her gaze rest on El Gris.

'It's you.'

El Gris said nothing, but Amparo detected a slight change in him. His breathing, his expression, betrayed . . . a sense of uncertainty perhaps, regret even?

'Do not harm my son. He doesn't deserve it,' Manuela continued. 'I know you are not a cruel man, despite everything. I know that the sensitive young man you were is still inside somewhere and . . .'

'Stop it,' El Gris interrupted. 'That boy died years ago. You killed him, when you treated him like a monster. You made me what I am today.'

'I didn't mean to . . .'

'But you did,' he interrupted her again. 'The only way to get back the person I was is to hand these two over to the wayfarer.'

Donna Manuela shook her head. 'I have no idea who this wayfarer is, but do you truly want to harm these innocent children?'

El Gris made no reply.

'After all the pain you have inflicted, all the families you have stolen children from . . .' Donna Manuela closed her eyes briefly. 'I am partly to blame for what you have done. You are right. If I had accepted you then for what you are, ignoring your appearance, we would not be here today.'

'At least we agree on something.' El Gris turned to address Amparo. 'Get in.'

Before Amparo could turn back towards the carriage, she heard someone shout, 'Watch out! He's got a knife!'

She looked around. 'Pepe?'

The imposing figure of Trastamara had suddenly materialised through the open gate. One arm hung limply by his side while the other brandished a glinting object.

'Claw!' Amparo screamed when she saw the man lunge at the panther.

The animal leapt instinctively, but the chains around its legs kept it pinned to the ground. Ester threw herself at Amparo, pulling her away. Trastamara pounced on the panther with a primal roar and, in an instant, man and beast were locked in a furious struggle, amid a cacophony of screams, snarling and hissing. They careened uncontrollably down the slope, sliding dangerously between the road and the fields.

Amparo, heedless of the danger, wrestled free of Ester and followed them.

'Wait!' a voice behind screamed. 'No, Amparo!'

The girl ignored Pepe's calls and raced after Claw. Each step was a struggle, the chains on her ankles causing her to stumble and lurch. She sprang over the road, landing heavily on the cold, hard clods of earth. A sharp pain pierced her ankle, but she pushed through it, sprinting as fast as she could towards Trastamara and the panther, the two locked in a fierce battle, surrounded by a cacophony of roars and shouts.

Then, in a heartbeat, the struggle ceased. The panther lay sprawled, its muzzle buried in the earth, Trastamara's bulky, awkward form slumped on top.

'No . . .'

Amparo ran to them, followed by Donna Manuela and Pepe. Upon seeing the bodies, he threw his arms up, beseeching the heavens above and any saint he could muster.

'Tomás!' Donna Manuela wailed, trying to push Trastamara off. Amparo, Pepe and Ester helped her, shoving with all their might until they finally managed to move him.

Amparo screamed when her eyes met the man's glassy stare. Trastamara was dead, killed by his own dagger, the blade driven deep into his heart during the frantic clash.

'Claw . . .' The girl leaned over the panther. She lay a hand on the animal's side, feeling for a heartbeat, a sign of movement, anything to prove her friend was still alive. Nothing.

Donna Manuela kneeled beside her and stroked the panther's head. 'Tomás? Tomás, it's me. Your mother.'

They heard steps behind them. Turning, Amparo saw that El Gris had caught up with them. He was no longer holding the rifle and, despite the dark, she could tell the expression on his face conveyed one thing and one thing only: sadness.

He scrabbled over into the field and stood by Donna Manuela's feet. She looked up at him and Amparo saw anger, pain and contempt on her face.

'Are you happy now? You've got what you wanted. He's dead.'

El Gris did not move, his narrow eyes locked on the panther.

'I want to speak with the wayfarer,' Donna Manuela said. 'I want to offer my life in place of Tomás's.'

This seemed to shake El Gris. 'No.'

'It's not up to you to decide what I do with my life, Julio,' she retorted.

'Julio . . .' he echoed in a distant, dreamy voice. 'Yes, I used to be Julio.'

'Take me to his wayfarer,' Donna Manuela insisted.

El Gris shook his head. 'No, I can't. I don't want to.'

The woman dug a finger into his chest. 'What you want is irrelevant. I want to speak to him!' She burst into tears. 'Please. I'm begging you . . .'

El Gris squeezed Donna Manuela's hand and something changed in him. For a second, Amparo thought she saw his cruel, hard features soften.

The door of the carriage suddenly flew open.

'Good God in Heaven above!' exclaimed Pepe. 'Who on earth is this now?'

A tall figure, wrapped in a long, black cape, face concealed under the hood and carrying a cane, climbed out of the carriage.

'Wasn't it empty?' Amparo mumbled.

The wayfarer approached the group. Pepe took a step back, scared, pulling Amparo into him. Ester placed herself in front of the two children, fearful, but the new arrival seemed to have eyes solely for El Gris and Donna Manuela.

Similar to what Pepe had just done, El Gris pulled Manuela closer. The wayfarer stopped facing the pair and reached out. From the voluminous sleeve of his cloak, a pale, delicate hand emerged, more like that of a skeleton. El Gris seemed to understand the silent request and handed over the last two remaining figurines. The wayfarer took them and crumbled them with his fingers, like brittle chalk. The dust and tiny fragments of wood were whisked away into the air by a gust of wind, like pollen, before they could scatter to the ground. The wayfarer then took a step towards the panther. He stood, motionless, observing it.

'That's my son,' Donna Manuela said. 'Please, save him if you can. Do whatever you can. Take my life instead, for what it's worth.'

The wayfarer held out his emaciated hand to Donna Manuela, and she took it without a second's hesitation. El Gris placed himself between them.

'No,' he said. 'This is between us. Let's finish it now. I renounce Julio Alameda. That man no longer exists for me.'

The wayfarer tipped his head to one side and studied El Gris, as if weighing his words. Amparo and Pepe clung to each other.

'When all this is over,' mumbled Pepe, 'if I make it through alive, I'll have me a bath in the holy water font. Because I'll be damned if that's not the devil himself!'

El Gris pushed Donna Manuela's arm down. Her hand slipped out of the wayfarer's grasp. A ferocious gust of wind swept across the field. The wayfarer took another step towards the panther and his cloak billowed out like a great black sail, momentarily concealing the feline beneath.

Almost as soon as it had started, the wind stopped and the cloak fell to his sides again.

'Heavenly Father above, have mercy on us!' Pepe whimpered.

The panther had vanished.

Lying in his place was a dark-haired boy. Alive. Chest rising and falling to the rhythm of his very much beating heart.

Donna Manuela kneeled on the ground, hugging Tomás to her chest, wrapping him in her shawl.

'Thank you,' she said, raising her head to look at El Gris. She gave him a smile.

The wayfarer turned to Amparo. He pointed his stick at Tomás then at her. She stepped back, frightened by the man, but more so by the choice he was offering her: to give up her life as an animal.

To no longer be a falcon would mean no longer seeing the world from above; it would mean renouncing the feeling of being free, the chance to live without limits or constraints, even for only part of the day, even if it meant never being fully part of one or the other world; to be half human, half animal, and all the suffering and fatigue this brought with it.

Pepe had also understood the wayfarer's silent question.

'You could have friends again,' he whispered. 'Go back to school, go to the beach, do the things that people – normal people – do.'

Amparo looked at him. 'I know. But . . .'

'But what?'

'I wouldn't feel whole if I lost the falcon part of me,' she said quietly. She looked up. 'No.'

If her answer took him by surprise, the wayfarer did not show it. He merely lowered his stick and nodded at El Gris to follow him.

Taking one last look at Donna Manuela and without asking questions or raising objections, El Gris fell silently into step behind the wayfarer. As they neared the bend, they vanished into a gentle cloud of dust that was carried away on the soft night breeze.

EPILOGUE

The rugged, towering silhouette of Puig Campana rose sharply against the glowing orange sky, its contours resembling the powerful, curved back of a sleeping bull. The priest had never been asked to hold a funeral at sunset before, but when the dark-haired boy with the slightly flat nose had come to him with the request, he agreed willingly. He had liked the boy immediately. He couldn't say the same, however, for the boy's sidekick, a street urchin with a little too much to say for himself and the unseemly habit of frequently invoking the Almighty, confidently asserting he had a 'direct line to the divine'.

When the ceremony was over, three people remained around the grave: the dark-haired boy, the street urchin, who had a falcon on his shoulder, and a beautiful woman with honey-coloured hair. The priest bid them farewell, shook the hand of the raven-haired boy, then set off for the village, heading back to the rectory.

The two children and the woman lingered a few more minutes until the woman cleared her throat.

'I'll see you at the cart.'

'Okay, Ester,' Tomás replied.

The air was beginning to cool as the sun started its slow

descent towards the horizon. The falcon soared away, in search of a safe, quiet spot outside the cemetery, beyond the trees. When the last traces of the sun's rays had gone, Amparo walked back into the cemetery, fastening her sage-coloured cape around her neck.

Tomás dug his hands into his trouser pockets and glanced up. 'I can't get used to seeing the night sky through human eyes.' He smiled. 'It's so beautiful.'

'Do you miss it?'

'What?'

'The panther.'

Tomás shook his head. 'No. For me it always felt like a prison, not a gift. Unlike for you.' He nodded at Amparo.

'Giving up being a falcon would have meant losing an important part of myself. I would've felt incomplete. And . . .' she shook her head, trying to articulate her thoughts, 'if I can't love myself for who I am, how can I expect anyone else to?'

'Er, love might be jumping the gun a bit, but, just so you know, I think you're great exactly as you are,' Pepe declared, his gaunt cheeks turning deep crimson in the process.

'Oh, that's a declaration of love if ever I heard one.' Tomás laughed.

'It is not!' Pepe cried, cheeks almost purple now. 'Actually,' he stated, turning to Amparo with a mock irritated air, 'if you want to continue travelling on this here shoulder, might I ask that you trim them there claws. They've scratched me to bits.'

'I'll see to it,' Amparo replied calmly.

'I sincerely hope so,' Pepe retorted. He looked at Tomás. 'And you can stop laughing. By the way, when does your ship set sail?'

'Midnight.'

'Do you know where to go, when you get to Marseille?'

'Amparo, you asked me that already,' replied Tomás, sounding a little exasperated but also a little amused. 'I've got the address my father's old friend gave me, you know, the pharmacist in Sagunto. And I know my mother's name and surname: Beatriz Castillo. There can't be that many Spanish families in Marseille, it should be easy to find mine.'

'If you had me with you, it would be,' Pepe proclaimed. 'But you on your own . . . ? Make sure you get on the right ship, you might find yourself who knows where otherwise, in Italy or Greece perhaps.'

The three friends erupted in uproarious laughter, dissolving the last remnants of tension. Two women dressed in black, who had just entered the cemetery, looked over disapprovingly.

'We'd best leave,' Amparo suggested.

'I need just a little longer,' Tomás said.

Amparo nodded, understanding. 'That's fine.'

She and Pepe left the cemetery, allowing Tomás the time to say goodbye to the woman who'd raised, loved and protected him for ten years.

'Have you spoken to your grandfather?' Pepe asked as they waited for their friend.

'Yes, before I came here.'

'And?'

'He really didn't know anything about my parents, other than what Donna Manuela told him the night of the Trastamara fire when she brought me to his house.'

'You mean, the fact that your parents were dead, and he was never to ask any questions if he didn't want you to end up the same way?'

Amparo nodded.

Pepe kicked a stone. 'I'm sorry. Trastamara deserved everything that happened to him.'

'Yes. Every single thing.'

Pepe cleared his throat. 'Listen, I never had the guts to ask Tomás, but . . .'

'What?'

'Before she died, did Donna Manuela ever explain why she went to the Trastamara place that night?'

'She believed El Gris was heading there,' Amparo replied.

'Why?'

'The Mother Superior had been tracking his movements, as far as she was able, that is, going by the reports of missing children and the locations where each disappearance had occurred. She knew he was in Valencia because he'd called into the convent asking about children adopted around 1900. She'd kicked him out and warned Donna Manuela, who was in the city at the time. If there was anyone who could make El Gris, or Julio Alameda rather, see sense, it was Donna Manuela.'

'El Gris didn't go to the Trastamaras though.'

'Tomás wasn't the only adopted child potentially of interest to El Gris,' Amparo explained. 'There were others, the Mother Superior told Donna Manuela. So Tomás was lucky, at least in that respect.'

Tomás joined them at that moment, deep sadness in his eyes.

'I feel like a traitor for leaving.'

'She's at peace now,' Amparo consoled him.

'And she's finally home,' Pepe added, pointing to the tiny village before them.

Silence hung heavily in the air, interrupted only by the sound of the wind rustling the leaves and the solitary hoot of a distant owl.

'By the way,' Pepe resumed, 'when you find your family in Marseille, you're not going to stay there, turn all French and forget about us, are you?'

Tomás looked at Pepe first then turned to look at Amparo.

'I could never forget you two.'

Amparo wrapped her arms around him in a burst of warmth and affection and Tomás, initially caught off guard, hugged her back.

'Hey, I'm here too!' cried Pepe, throwing himself at the pair.

'Children, it's time to go!' called Ester, holding a lantern by the carriage. 'Tomás might miss the ship!'

The three friends broke apart, releasing their embrace. On their way over to the carriage, a young couple crossed their path, a little older than the three, walking hand in hand and giggling together affectionately.

'Excuse me, does this path go to the abandoned village?' the boy asked.

Tomás hesitated. 'Yes, but . . .'

'It's not a nice place,' Amparo intervened. 'I wouldn't go there if I were you.'

'We're not scared of ghosts,' the girl stated.

'Ghosts are the least you'd have to worry about in that place,' Pepe remarked.

The couple exchanged a confused glance then, after a hasty and somewhat confused 'thank you', continued on their way.

'Let's hope they take our advice,' Pepe sighed.

'Do you think he's still there?' Amparo asked.

'Who?' said Tomás.

'The wayfarer,' replied Amparo.

'No way,' Pepe said firmly. 'You saw it too, didn't you? He vanished with El Gris into thin air.'

'What do you think he was?' Amparo asked.

'Some questions are better not asked,' Pepe declaimed, hopping up on to the cart. 'Unless you can cope with the answers. And after everything we've been through, I'm not sure I could.'

'Such wisdom,' Ester commented. She waited for Amparo and Tomás to climb aboard then clicked her tongue. The horse neighed and set off, swishing its long tail this way and that to swat away the flies.

The cart trundled along the road to Valencia, skirting the village. Rocked by the gentle swaying of the cart and mesmerised by the stars beginning to fill the sky, the three were unaware of the dark silhouette observing them from the top of the hill.

When the cart disappeared round a bend, the solitary figure reached a hand into the pocket of its long black cape and pulled out something shiny: a golden key. Holding it between his slender fingers, he turned around and, with one final glance at the spot where the cart had disappeared from view, set off towards the abandoned village.

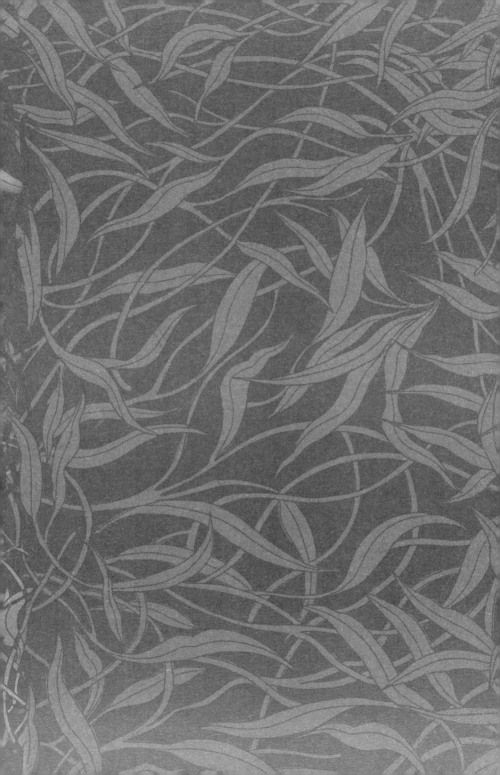